Magnolia Blossom

By

Joanne Fisher

Acknowledgements

Copyright© 2020 by Joanne Fisher. All Rights Reserved.

This is a work of historical fiction. Names, characters, businesses, places, events, locales, and incidents are either the products of the author's imagination or used in a fictitious manner. Any resemblance to actual persons, living or dead, or actual events is purely coincidental.

Author: Joanne Fisher

Published by Joanne's Books

Cover design by MacRed Designs, Inc.

Edited by Daniel B. Fisher

Author photograph by Daniel B. Fisher

ISBN: 978-1-7923-4003-1 (Paperback)

Special Thanks

A special Thank You goes out to historical advisor James Permane. James is a Civil War re-enactor who began studying the Civil War as a youth. He has provided tremendous support and assistance in the writing of this novel.

Other Novels by Joanne Fisher

With All of Me I

With All of Me II

Her Spanish Doll

Good Things Always Happen in Springtime

Traveling Boomers – First Stop Italy

Baker's Dozen Anthology

The Devil of St. Gabriel

Christmas in Venice

Dedication

To my biggest fan on earth, my sister, Carolina. She has been where I have been and sometimes knows me better than I know myself. She is not just family, she is my best friend, my guiding light, and my confidant. The closeness we have shared through life's joys and tears is like having a warm blanket to wrap myself up in. I am blessed to have a sister like her. She is a kindred spirit and she will always be there for me as I will be for her. She is the best kind of sister…my sister.

Foreword

Although this novel is a work of historical fiction, the author has done painstaking research into the Civil War, its battles, and the lifestyles of the plantation owners and their slaves, to make it as realistic as possible. There is language in here that, quite frankly, is foreign and potentially offensive to most twenty-first century Americans. The author attempted to recapture the speech and mannerisms of the mid-Nineteenth Century as accurately as possible, given the constraints of modern American English, into which the words and speaking parlance of that era do not fit well. Slavery was and is an evil that needed to be stamped out. However, it is fact that, while many—perhaps even most—slaveowners mistreated and abused their slaves, many treated them with dignity and respect, understanding that slavery is immoral and that people work better when they're not abused. The author hopes that you will enjoy this novel. It must be emphasized, in no uncertain terms, that she abhors slavery, prejudice, and discrimination in all its forms, and nothing herein should be construed otherwise.

Chapter One

Maggie Mae paced up and down the hallway waiting for the doctor to come out of her parent's room. What seemed like an eternity, was only a few minutes. Finally, Dr. Johnson came out of the room, closing the door behind him. He wiped the sweat from his brow and placed his handkerchief back into the pocket of his brocade coat, which was of the best imported fabric from Paris.

"Doctor, how are they?"

He shook his head. "I'm afraid it's not good, child."

"Whatever do you mean?"

"They both have dysentery. Neither one has much time to live. I'm sorry." He placed his stethoscope into his black leather bag. "Now, you need to get your affairs in order and please, keep all children out of that room, ya hear?"

"But doctor, how did they contract it? And both of them? How horrible!" She couldn't believe her ears.

She quivered and felt ill to her stomach. She felt her corset tighten under her plaid, wool antebellum outfit.

"They contracted it from another infected person." As he spoke, Dr. Johnson descended the live oak stairway covered with handmade Turkish runner. "Tell me, did you have anybody come to visit lately?"

Maggie Mae followed him down the stairs. "Why no, doctor. They've been sick for a while now."

"I see. Well, did they go slave shoppin' lately?" He had arrived at the front heavy oak door. The entrance was fairly large with two stained glass windows on each side of the masterfully built door. The doctor took his hat from the rot iron hook and gently rubbed the inside rim as if to clean it.

"Well…" She hesitated. "The last time they went to the slave market was about two months prior."

The doctor placed his hat on his head. "There you have it. They must have come in contact with a sick slave. Dysentery is a very contagious disease nowadays. They're bringin' back all sorts of sick slaves from the black continent, and Lord only knows what kind of diseases they're carryin'!" He opened the front door. "I'm very sorry, my dear. I'll stop by again in a few days." He tipped his hat and left. She slowly closes the door behind him and entered the salon. Memories came flooding into her head. There was his favorite chair and there was her mother embroidering a pillow case that was part of Maggie Mae's dowry.

"Oh, my goodness, what are we to do?" she asked as Flora approached. She felt faint and wobbled to the nearest chair.

"I dunno, Missy Maggie." She put down her feather duster and helped her mistress to the armchair. "Can I getcha sum tea?" She knelt in front of Maggie Mae.

"I told daddy not to buy that sick boy slave, but he didn't listen. 'We'll make him better,' he said. 'He'll be fine in no time.' He said. Well, daddy, you were so wrong." She hid her face in her hands and wept.

Fanny let her cry for a few seconds, then pulled her hands apart. "Missy Maggie, now, you mus' be strong, ya heah? Ya must be strong for your parents and yo' childr'n and yo' husband." She scurried to the kitchen. "I'll make ya sum tea quicker than green…"

She always tried to bring laughter into Maggie Mae's life, but now wasn't the time, so she hastily left her on the sofa, crying and wiping her eyes with her handkerchief.

Roland passed Flora, as he entered the salon. He was tall, handsome and seemed to have not changed a bit since he first laid eyes on her. When he saw his wife weeping, he knelt in front of her. "My darling, why the tears?"

She hugged him. The only thing she wanted was to feel the tight grip of her by her beloved husband's arms.

"There, there, my love. Tell me, what is it?"

"The doctor said both mama and daddy are going to die." She was whaling now. "Oh, Lord! Why both of them? Why?"

"Oh, I am so sorry, my love." He lifted her chin to meet her eyes. "I will be here. I'm not going anywhere. I will help you with this plantation. Please be strong, my love, be strong." He didn't know what else to say. He had no words of comfort. All he could do for the moment was to hold her and be there.

Jonas, Flora's husband, limped into the salon and removed his hat. He waited, hoping the couple would notice him, but ended up clearing his throat after a moment.

"Oh, Jonas." Maggie dried her eyes. "What is it?"

"Well, Missy Maggie, the young boy done passed just a few minutes ago."

"Oh, how tragic! Such a youngin'." She burst out crying again, the wounds too fresh to cover.

Roland shook his head. The lad was a negro. He would never understand his wife's tender heart for them.

"Yes, Missy. He was too young." Jonas stared a hole through the rug.

Forcibly, Maggie stood and took a deep breath. "Well, I suppose we'll have to bury him. Would you mind?"

"No, Missy Maggie Mae I don't mind at all."

"I'll help you, Jonas," Roland said, placing a strong arm around his wife's shoulders.

"Much appreciated, Mr. Moon."

Maggie Mae smiled at Roland. He was always there for her, since the very beginning. He was different than her other contenders. She still didn't know why. Perhaps his tenderness towards her or perhaps his gentleness even though he was very muscular or perhaps his silence during these times. She faced Jonas. "Thank you again, Jonas. Please bury him in the black-folk graveyard and don't let any of the children help you. You best be covering your faces. He may still be contagious."

"Yes, Missy. Do y'all want me to have Charles say a few words?"

"Why yes, that would be fine." She sat back down. "Oh, and please have everyone on the plantation attend. I want him to have a proper sendin' off."

"Yes, ma'am." Jonas slightly bowed, before turning on his heel and exiting the manor. What a wonderful man Flora married. Of all the slaves, he was the gentlest with her family.

Maggie kissed Roland's cheek. "I best be changing my dress then." She climbed the ornate stairs, carefully placing each step as grief tried to buckle her knees. The long, familiar hallway was adorned with antiques, silver candles, and hanging mirrors in frames. Her bedroom was warm, filled with family heirlooms and trinkets from childhood. She always felt safe within these walls, like the world couldn't enter it. Until today. She pushed back her tears as she called for her maid, Flora, then sat at her vanity. As she removed her jewelry, Flora tapped on the oak door and peered inside.

"You called for me, Misses?"

"Come in Flora."

"Yes, Miss Magnolia May. Thank you," she said as she closed the door quietly behind her.

Flora and Maggie Mae had grown up together. They were best friends, even though the Terrys did not approve of their closeness, and the two girls were inseparable as children and teenagers. This continued even after they both married and had children of their own. Flora knew her position well, yet she would always be Maggie's best friend and confidant.

"Please, Flora, call me Maggie. There's nobody around anyway."

"All right, Maggie." She helped her mistress unbutton her pretty, colorful dress. "Will you wear your black dress?"

"Yes. That new boy slave passed, and I need to prepare for the sendin'."

"Yes, w'all heard that." Flora shook her head. "How sad. He was such a sweet boy, but so sick…how unfortunate."

Flora hung the colorful dress on a hanger and placed it in the large armoire. She removed the black antebellum dress layered with lace and silk bows, the black petticoat for beneath, and a pair of long, black gloves with matching bonnet. She brought them to Maggie Mae. "How are your mama and daddy doin'?"

"Not good, Flora, not good at all. Doctor says they're both gonna die and that I have to get their affairs in order."

"Oh, my Lord! I am so sorry, Maggie!" Tears filled her dark eyes. The Terrys were like a second set of parents to her. She was never treated as a slave in this family. "What can I do to help ya?"

"Nothin' really. We just need to wait."

"And the doctor cain't do nothin'?"

"No. He's done everything he could." Her lip trembled as tears threatened to fall. Maggie Mae took a deep breath to compose herself.

As Flora finished up dressing her mistress, she had to dry her eyes too.

"Flora, please prepare my children as well. I'll meet y'all at the gravesite."

"Yes, Maggie." She left as quietly as she had entered.

When Maggie Mae had shed her last tear, for the time being at least, she made her way to the gravesite. Slowly, all the slaves, her husband, and her children joined her. When everyone was gathered and in silence, Charles began to speak.

"Beloved, we are gathered here today to say our goodbyes to this young slave boy who arrived at the end of summer, very sick. He never got better. I do not know his name. Does anyone know his name?" He looked around only to see heads shaking. "Well, all right then, I'll name him George, like our state." He opened his Bible. "In the words of Jesus: Let not your heart be troubled: ye believe in God, believe also in me. In my Father's house are many mansions: if it were not so, I would have told you. I go to prepare a place for you. And if I go and prepare a place for you, I will come again, and receive you unto myself; that where I am, there ye may be also. And whither I go ye know, and the way ye know. Amen."

The crowd murmured as one, "Amen."

"Now, I don't know if this young child ever accepted God in his heart but since he was so young, I pray the good Lord to accept him into heaven. Let us pray."

Obediently, the group bowed their heads.

"Father, thank you so much for your grace and your goodness, for your message of hope, for this young child's life. We thank you that he is now safe in your presence and we pray that today, you fill us with faith, and guide us along our way, so that we might end up in the same place when it is our time. In Jesus' name, Amen."

"Amen," came the unison voice of the bystanders. Then Charles led the way, and every person followed suit, taking a handful of dirt, and tossing it in the grave. The last person to throw the dirt was Maggie.

"Thank you, Charles. That was very moving." She patted his arm as she passed.

"It was nothin' really. Poor boy. His life was too short."

"Well, prepare for another two funerals because mama and daddy are next." Tears welled as she joined hands with her beloved husband.

"Oh, Missy Maggie Mae, I am so sorry," he said as he too, became emotional.

The Terrys did not deserve to die.

George Paul Terry and Anita Sarah Terry were not your run of the mill slaveowners. They treated their slaves with dignity and respect. Their neighboring slaveowners often criticized them because of their lenience. Charles would often recall how, when the Terrys had a party, their guests would badmouth the slaves and call them terrible names. But George and Anita would scold their guests, who would end up leaving because they became offended by such behavior.

"I will not tolerate such conduct," George always said.

He didn't even like being *called* a slaveowner. As far as he was concerned, he was a landowner and his slaves were his workers.

After several years and after they properly married off their daughter, the many failed parties began to dwindle until George and Anita rarely entertained. Their only outing became church on Sunday mornings and weekly trips into Valdosta for supplies.

Now, they were never going anywhere again.

Almost exactly to the month, on a bright and crisp November morning, Anita passed. During that month, Maggie had the older slave boys dig two graves and she had the slave men build two coffins. She had no choice but to have Reverend Macy perform the service, even though she preferred Charles, but it was not proper for a slave to perform burial services for their masters. Another social norm that the Terrys didn't like. So reluctantly, she sent Roland to fetch the reverend with the horse and carriage.

"Daddy, are you well enough to come to Mama's burial?"

He nodded. "Please, can you have the workers carry me to the gravesite?"

"Yes, daddy, I would be happy to." She kissed her father on his forehead. How strong he was. She was going to miss him so, and the sadness crippled her desire to do anything more than sit on her bed and cry. But she had to be strong, for her parents and her children.

Around one o'clock that afternoon, all the white folk gathered at the gravesite with Maggie Mae up front by her father, husband, and two children. Her father sat uncomfortably in the chair that the slaves had brought for him. The slaves had to stay in a group behind all the white folk. They weren't allowed to interact with the white folk at all. The Terrys didn't like that; they would have preferred the slaves to be with them, but this wasn't the time to spark a neighborhood feud.

The reverend began the burial ceremony.

"We are gathered here today to bid farewell to our sister, Anita Sarah Terry. She has lived a life of righteousness and always remained faithful to our Lord and Savior. Bow your heads and pray." He paused a moment, then continued. "I am the resurrection and the life, saith the Lord; he that believeth in me, though he were dead, yet shall he live; and whosoever liveth and believeth in me shall never die. I know that my Redeemer liveth, and that he shall stand at the latter day upon the earth; and though this body be destroyed, yet shall I see God; whom I shall see for myself and mine eyes shall behold, and not as a stranger. For none of us liveth to himself, and no man dieth to himself. For if we live, we live unto the Lord, and if we die, we die unto the Lord. Whether we live, therefore, or die, we are the Lord's." Then he picked up a handful of dirt. "All flesh shall perish together, and man shall turn again into dust." He opened his hand and the dirt slowly rained upon the coffin. "Oh, Lord, lift your faithful servant's spirit up to paradise to reside by your side forever and ever, in Jesus' name we pray, Amen."

Once the funeral ceremony was finished and all the white folk had made their way to the main house along with the reverend, the slaves could approach the grave and give their last respects.

Maggie Mae was in no mood to hold a burial gathering but she had to keep up face, so she entertained all close family, neighbors, and friends until one by one, they all left. As soon as she saw the last guest leave the front gate with their horse and carriage, she called the slaves to come and eat the rest of the food. She detested wasting food. After everyone had eaten, they began to clean up and by nightfall, the house looked like nobody had been there. Now, Maggie Mae was free to cry alone in her room. Roland thought it be best to leave her be, so he decided to retire in the guest bedroom.

It was December first, and Maggie had the Christmas decorations pulled from the attic. She hadn't even opened the first box when Charles again stood at the entrance of the sitting room with his hat in his hand.

"Missy Maggie?"

"Yes, Charles?" She continued working on the box of decorations.

"Best to put those decorations away."

She looked up. "Daddy!" and took off like a rocket to his room.

Chapter Two

Maggie Mae was tired of wearing black all the time, but the traditional mourning period was at least a month and, seeing that she'd lost both parents not even within a month of each other, the mourning period needed to be longer. It was the proper thing to do.

It was an extraordinarily warm March morning when the letterman pulled up and gave Roland an envelope. He quickly went in the house. "My darling, we received this letter today." Roland held the envelope up.

"All right, well, go ahead and open it." She sat down, nervously, hoping against hope that it wasn't more unwelcome news.

He pulled out a silver letter opener from the roll-top desk and carefully opened the envelope, pulled out the parchment, and silently read. "It's from your father's lawyer."

She knew it was regarding his Will. "Continue, please."

"Dear Mr. and Mrs. Moon. Your presence is requested at our offices for the reading of the Last Will and Testament of George Paul Terry."

"Oh, I was waiting for this. What day and time?"

"March eighteenth, eighteen-hundred and sixty-one, ten o'clock a.m."

"Very well then, we must attend."

"Oh, but darling, they were your parents, not mine."

"I understand but your name was also mentioned, wasn't it?"

"Yes, it was."

"Well, then, we are both going to Valdosta, and that's final."

~~~~~~

At nine-forty-five a.m., they both entered the offices of Gable and Sons, on Main Street. The anteroom was modestly appointed, with two sitting chairs—not extremely ornate, but very comfortable—and a small side table in between. The fragrance of expensive cigar smoke lightly permeated the room.

"Oh, Mr. and Mrs. Moon. How are y'all doin' today?"

Roland shook the hands of a strong, young Douglas Gable, youngest son of Timothy Gable. "Doing well, Mr. Gable. Doing well, considering the circumstances."

Douglas was a young, slender man with dark hair. He was somewhat muscular, appearing to be physically active. He was dressed in a two-piece suit with a necktie that wasn't tied tightly enough. His shirt wasn't quite tucked in properly, and his jacket was unbuttoned. Maggie was not impressed. She wondered about Douglas's education. She wondered what would happen to the Timothy's law practice when he passed on and turned it over to Douglas.

Nevertheless, Maggie extended her gloved hand to be kissed by the young man., who kissed it respectfully, "Well, Mr. Gable, you have turned into a mighty fine young man."

"Why, thank you, ma'am." The younger Mr. Gable blushed, slightly. He began walking toward the back office where his father was waiting. "Right this way, please."

Timothy Gable's office was rather ornate. The odor of cigar smoke was much more pronounced in here than in the anteroom. The office walls were covered with somewhat faded gold wallpaper with swirl designs. A bookshelf filled with various law books took up an entire wall. The books were all lined up, in almost perfect order.

Mr. Gable sat in a large, somewhat-worn leather high-backed chair behind a huge oak desk, with ornate carvings. Two obviously used, but still quite comfortable chairs were placed in front of, and facing, the desk.

Timothy Gable was an imposing man, somewhat rotund. He was still very handsome at almost fifty, with silver streaks in his hair, chestnut eyes, and dressed elegantly, such as a lawyer would be dressed. He had a loud, booming voice. He got up from his chair, removed a half-smoked cigar from his mouth, set it in the ashtray, and said, "Welcome! Please! Make yourselves comfortable. Mrs. Moon, how lovely to see you again. How are you holding up?" He kissed her hand, almost reverently.

"I'm doing just fine. As well as one might expect, Mr. Gable. Thank you."

"Mr. Moon, how about yourself?" they men shook hands.

"Doin' all right."

He looked at Roland, holding a box of the finest imported cigars. "Cigar?"

"No, thanks."

"All right; you can't say that I didn't offer!"

Once they were all settled into their seats, Timothy opened the top drawer of his massive oak desk and removed a small stack of papers.

"Before we begin, please allow me to express my deepest condolences on behalf of myself and my entire family. Your parents were one of a kind, indeed, Miss Maggie Mae."

"Thank you kindly, Mr. Gable."

"Well, all right then." He cleared his throat. "You obviously know why you're here."

They both nodded.

Timothy Gable adjusted his spectacles, lifted the papers slightly from the desktop, and began to read.

I, George Paul Terry, a legal resident of Lowndes County, State of Georgia, being of sober and sound mind, do hereby make and publish this as my true Last Will and Testament, revoking all other wills heretofore made by me.

First: I will and bequeath my body to Our Heavenly Father, who gave it to me, and I offer my soul to the Lord Jesus Christ, and I desire that after my death my body shall be buried in a decent manner and that all of my funeral and burial expenses and my doctor's bills and all other of my just debts be paid out of my personal estate by my executors, hereinafter named.

Second: I will and bequeath all of my estate, both personal and real to the following named party, to-wit; Anita Sarah Terry, who is my lawful wedded wife. Should my wife, Anita Sarah Terry, not survive me, I leave all of my personal and real property to my son-in-law, Roland David Moon, on the condition that he keep my one and only daughter, Magnolia Mae Moon, his lawful wedded wife, not wanting of anything until the day she shall pass away. Should Roland David Moon predecease Magnolia Mae Moon, or should the marriage of Magnolia Mae Moon and Roland David Moon end for whatever other reason, I leave all of my personal and real property to my one and only daughter, Magnolia Mae Moon, on the condition that she keep the estate known as Magnolia Blossom Plantation maintained in pristine condition for her children and her children's children.

Given under my hand this Twentieth day of August, in the year of our Lord, 1846.

Signed, George Paul Terry

"Well, I'll be!" Roland was flabbergasted, to say the least.

"I knew there was a good reason for you to come in today," Maggie Mae remarked, smiling.

"Indeed," Timothy interjected. "From the looks of it, your father-in-law really loved you like his own."

"I-I-I suppose he did," he stammered, "I mean, I knew that he thought highly of me; he always told me that I was the best thing that ever happened to Maggie Mae. But—but—I never expected anything like this!"

"Well, Mr. Gable, is that all?" Maggie Mae asked.

"Not quite, Mrs. Moon. I will require Mr. Moon's signature on this heah piece of paper." He slid the document to Roland, who turned it, dipped the pen into the inkwell, and signed on the line.

"There you are, Mr. Gable." Roland stood.

"Very good. But before you go, I have an inquiry for y'all."

"Yes, Mr. Gable?"

"Well, Mr. Moon, I would strongly suggest that you prepare a Last Will and Testament of your own."

"Why would you suggest that, Mr. Gable?"

"Well, there's a war a-goin' on right now and you could be called for duty any day."

"Yes, the war. I forgot about that." He looked at his wife, who returned a warm smile. "Well, all right then." He sat back down. "Would now be all right, sir?"

"Oh, yes, of course. But I will need at least an hour to draw up the document."

"That's quite all right, Mr. Gable," Maggie Mae said. "Roland needs to buy some seed and I'm pressed to find some other things. We'll be back in one hour."

"Thank you, Mrs. Moon. Much obliged."

Once out on the street, the Moons went their separate ways. Roland needed seeds and Maggie Mae wanted to find some new fabric at the general store. Around one, they met at their favorite place, The Valdosta Saloon.

The saloon was rather typical for the time. The odor of stale cigar and pipe smoke lingered in the air. Eight or ten tables with mismatched chairs were arranged in the center of the dining area. Off to the left, as one entered, was the bar, with bottles of various and sundry distilled spirits on the shelf. The bar was polished to a fine sheen, so the barkeep could slide the drinks to the patrons. The floor was old and worn, but as clean as was possible.

"Mornin' folks. What can I get y'all today?" Mrs. Donnelly, who ran the saloon, asked. She pointed them to their favorite table, Of course Roland, being the gentleman that he was, held Maggie Mae's chair while she sat. Only after she was situated did he seat himself.

"We'll have some tea and some pie, please." Maggie removed her gloves and rested them on her lap.

"What pie do you have today?" Roland asked hoping for cherry, his favorite kind.

"Rhubarb."

I hate rhubarb! Roland said, "Two pieces, please."

"Now, don't pout, Roland. They'll have cherry next time."

He kissed her hand. "You are the most positive person I have ever met. How I love you, my darling." She blushed as he kissed her hand a second time.

Her stomach fluttered every time he did that, even all these years later. He had reddish-brownish curly hair with ample sideburns which he kept well groomed, emerald green eyes that stole her breath, and matching dimples on either side of his sculpted face. "Tell you what. I'll have Chesney bake you a cherry pie when we get home."

"Oh, darling, you are so extraordinary. How I love you so—with all of me!" He wanted to kiss her passionately, but it was not proper to do so in public.

"So do I, my love. —I love you with all of me, too!"

~~~~~~

Maggie Mae and Roland had met at her Debutante Ball, many years earlier. She was the most beautiful debutante there, with her white dress adorned in lace, pearls, and silk embroidery. Her curly, charcoal black hair, also laced with white pearls, fell upon her shoulders. Her father introduced her to the higher-ups in society, where she curtsied as she had practiced. He then took her over to Roland Moon. "Roland Moon, I'd like you to meet my daughter, Miss Magnolia Mae Terry. Magnolia Mae, this is Roland Moon, your escort for the evening." Roland was the son of a wealthy cotton merchant in Valdosta, with whom George had done business for years. George had known Roland since birth and knew how he had been raised. He always believed that Roland would be a worthy husband for his Maggie Mae.

Even though she wore long, satin gloves, Roland felt her warmth when he ever-so-lightly kissed her hand. Only a few days passed, before he asked George, "Mr. Terry, I am deeply in love with Magnolia Mae, and I would like to ask you for her hand in marriage."

"Well, you are an upstanding, God-fearing young man. I have known you as long as you have been alive. I give you my blessing to marry my daughter. However, you must wait until you are of age." On July 4, 1847, Roland Moon and Magnolia Mae Terry were married in the back yard of Magnolia Blossom Plantation, right under the Magnolia tree from whence Maggie Mae got her name. There were many picnic baskets lined up on the lawn, creating an isle leading to the arch that was adorned with many different kinds of Georgia flora like Fothergill, Ashe's calamint, Florida bellwort, wild coco, Little River Canyon Onion, and others.

Maggie Mae's bouquet was arranged with roses, pansies, hyacinths, and orange blossoms adorned her black, curly hair. Her snow-white gown was made of organdy and tulle with puffy mutton-leg sleeves and a bustled skirt. It was the first wedding gown sewn by Rose, showcasing her remarkable ability to create flamboyant masterpieces. As per the latest fashion, a cameo hung from a silver chain around her neck.

She was a splendid and mesmerizing bride. Roland, normally a very stoic man, was so overwhelmed that he had difficulty fighting back tears.

Pastor James Murphy, from Shiloh Baptist Church, officiated. "Roland David Moon, do you take Magnolia Mae Terry to be your lawfully wedded wife, to have and to hold, from this day forward, for richer, for poorer, for better or for worse, in sickness and health, as long as you both shall live?"

"I do."

"Magnolia Mae Terry, do you take Roland David Moon to be your lawfully wedded husband, to have and to hold, from this day forward, for richer, for poorer, for better or for worse, in sickness and health, as long as you both shall live?"

Maggie's voice cracked, slightly, but she was able to say, softly, as she looked deeply into Roland's eyes, "I do."

"By the power invested in me by Almighty God and the State of Georgia, I now pronounce you man and wife. You may kiss the bride." The entire assembly cheered as Mr. Moon took Mrs. Moon into his arms and kissed her passionately.

"Ladies and gentlemen, may I present Mr. and Mrs. Roland David Moon." Everyone applauded joyfully.

The reception was held in the extraordinarily large salon where the one large table was decked with a variety of foods prepared lovingly by the servants' hands. After dinner, all the furniture was moved, so as to accommodate the small orchestra. It was quite lavish, but since George had only one child, he wanted to go all out to make her special day memorable. Afterward, the couple moved in to Magnolia Blossom Plantation, where George had prepared the west wing for them.

~~~~~~

Maggie Mae smiled at the pleasant memory as Mrs. Donnelly brought the tea and pie, served her customers, and went on to the next table.

"Darling, will you be going to war?" Maggie asked the question almost imperceptibly, not really wanting to know the answer.

"It is not my intent. However, if they call me, I will have no choice."

"Well, that's not fair." She pouted. "You're a family man. And now, you have a plantation to run."

"Now, darlin', don't worry your sweet little heart. Everything will be fine."

"Fine? How can I possibly run the plantation without my husband? I'm certain the gov'ment will understand our situation."

"They might or they might not." He gently squeezed her hand. "Please don't worry about this now. We have pie and tea to think about."

Maggie Mae grinned as Roland's charm won out in the end.

After they finished their tea and pie, they headed to pick up the goods they had ordered earlier. Their wagon was filled with cotton seed, sugar cane, animal feed, various canned goods, and new fabric that had recently arrived.

The economy in Victorian Georgia was mainly agricultural, based mainly on plantations growing indigo, rice, and sugar—and especially, cotton. Most of Georgia's money came from these cash crops. Although slavery had been prohibited in the original charter of Georgia, constant complaints from the settlers resulted in a revised charter in 1751, allowing slavery. Cotton picking did not become plentiful until the cotton gin was invented in 1793.

"We're going to have an abundant crop this year," Roland said on their way home.

"Do you really think so?"

"Yes. Even if your daddy is gone, we can depend on our slaves--"

"Workers, Roland, workers," Maggie Mae interrupted. "I don't like the term slave."

"Fine. We can depend on our *workers* to expertly work the land like they've done in the past."

"Yes, I agree. They are very skillful, and they know our land inside and out. Daddy trusted their judgment very much, and I truly believe that it is for this reason we have always had an abundant crop."

"And I'll tell you another thing, Maggie. When I hear other slave owners talk about their slaves and how they're lazy good for nothins, well if you ask me, I think it is because of the way they are treated. You can beat a slave night and day, but you can't force 'em to do anythin' if they don't want to."

Roland had not been raised to treat slaves with decency. After having lived with the Terrys for so many years, though, he saw firsthand how much more dedicated and hardworking they were because the Terrys treated them with dignity and respect. Any one of them would die for a master like the Terrys. Roland wasn't going to stir the pot. Things worked fine the way they were, even though he detested calling them *workers*. But it was a small price to pay for having the loyalty and expertise of the slaves, he decided.

"I agree, my darling," Maggie Mae added. "My mama and daddy always treated their slaves with dignity and respect. Why, if it were for me, I would abolish slavery right now."

"Well, I wouldn't go that far, but you do have a point. If you treat them like half-human beings, you get more out of them." He didn't quite agree with his wife, but being in public, he knew not to create a scene.

"I was taught that kindness and compassion are the way to a person's heart," Maggie Mae said.

"So, true, darlin', so true."

~~~~~~

Over the next several months, the sadness and mourning slowly dissipated, like the fog on a winter's morning. Sunshine, in the form of happiness, again surrounded Magnolia Blossom Plantation. The seeds were sown and the right balance of rain and sunshine brought forth abundant crops. Roland would go out with the slaves and work the land as if he were one of them. Perhaps he worked harder because of the fact that he was the owner of this abundantly flourishing property. Roland was treated very well when he went to town to sell his crops. And he was a shrewd businessman too, able to haggle and get the best prices for his crops. This earned him great respect but also some jealousy among the other plantation owners.

Maggie Mae kept busy organizing entertainment venues for Thanksgiving, Christmas, Easter and midsummer barbecues, for all their friends and neighbors. She truly enjoyed entertaining her guests and it seemed that her guests also enjoyed attending her parties.

When Maggie went into town, whomever she encountered always had good things to say about her get-togethers. There were guessing games, word games, dominoes, backgammon, checkers, and chess. Not to mention, dancing. She would arrange a small orchestra to play all the songs that were popular at that time like *Das*

Pensionat, Down Among the Cane-Brakes, Mephisto Waltz, Teniers the Grimbergen, Susanna, The Old Folks at Home, Jeanie With the Light Brown Hair, and *Swedish Nightingale*. No longer walking in the shadows of her mother, she was now creating her own reputation as a fine plantation hostess.

Maggie Mae also wore the latest fashions well. Although she had birthed two children, her figure had remained quite slim. The dressmaker of the plantation, Rose, had been there before Maggie was born. She had created all of Anita's outfits, and now she worked on Maggie's wardrobe. It was sad for Rose to see Anita's clothing collecting dust, and if it were proper, she might have even asked her mistress if she could take a few of the older dresses and use them for herself. Rose had a gifted eye for design and measurements. All Maggie Mae had to do was show Rose the pictures of the models from the magazines she received from New York, and within two weeks, Rose would have the perfect copy of that outfit on Maggie Mae's bed. She would always compliment her when Rose completed any garment and Rose would always do her best to please her mistress.

Sometimes, Maggie Mae would have Rose accompany her when she went to Valdosta to buy fabric and notions. She wanted her opinion because Rose knew exactly how much fabric and notions to buy. Her exacting eye for measurements aided in not allowing the owner of the store to swindle Maggie Mae into buying more than she needed. This situation sometimes caused Mrs. Potters, the store owner to not allow Rose into her shop. Still, Maggie Mae found a way to obtain her opinion, even if she wasn't in the store.

One bitter cold day in November, when Roland had returned home from the market, he was met by Charles who was holding a letter.

"Good evening, Charles." He noticed the parchment in his hand. "Is that for me?"

"Yes, Massa…" He handed him the letter.

Roland looked it over and frowned. "Well, dang, this cannot be good." He huffed and shoved it inside his front jacket pocket.

They didn't say anything more, but they didn't have to. Both knew damn well who the sender was.

Chapter Three

To: Mr. Roland David Moon
Magnolia Blossom Plantation
Valdosta, Georgia
You are ordered to report, without undue delay, to the Reception Center in Charleston, South Carolina to begin formal training for the Army of the Confederate States of America.

"War?" Maggie Mae asked.

"Yes, darling. I've been drafted." He threw the letter on the bed in anger.

"But…but I thought married men didn't have to go."

"So did I, but seems the Confederacy needs able bodies for fightin' and I'm as able-bodied as they come."

He did have a point. Roland was trim, and as fit as the day they'd met. He wasn't thin; rather, he was quite muscular, especially since he worked the land alongside the slaves. He was also quite tall for a man from Irish lineage, thankfully without the temperament. His was a typical southern gentleman.

Maggie Mae's knees went suddenly weak. She quickly sat down in her bedroom armchair, to keep from wilting onto the floor. "Whatever will we do?" she cried out. "How will we manage without you? We won't be able to survive!" She felt emptiness an emptiness in her spirit that she'd never felt before. She buried her face in her open hands.

"Oh, my darling, please don't cry. You're goin' to be fine. Just fine. You'll see. Besides, you got plenty of sla- *workers* to work the land, and you got plenty of the workers' children that are coming of age." He knelt in front of her and moved her hands away from her face. "Come now, Maggie, my love, be courageous. You do understand there's nothing I can do. I must go."

She hugged her husband and kissed him passionately. "This won't be easy, Roland, not easy at all."

"I understand, my love, I do." Roland stood and took her hand. He opened his Bible. "Let us read: *For we know that if our earthly house of this tabernacle were dissolved, we have a building of God, a house not made with hands, eternal in the heavens....We are confident, I say, and willing rather to be absent from the body, and to be present with the Lord.*"

"Wherefore we labor, that, whether present or absent, we may be accepted of him...." They gazed into each other's eyes, comforted by the words. "Come now, we must gather the workers and tell them the news."

~~~~~~

December first was an extraordinarily warm day. Bright sunshine filled the world, but Maggie Mae's soul was filled with dark clouds. Her beloved had not yet left, but a hollowness already permeated her heart. Charles loaded Roland's bag onto the carriage as he said farewell to his children.

"Pauly, you're ten years old now, which makes you a man, and men don't cry. Ya heah?" Roland tried to stay strong as he addressed his son. Inside, his heart broke into pieces as he imagined the time that would pass until he would see his family again. The boy simply nodded. "Now, you promise yo' Daddy that you'll be the man of the house and take care of yo' mothuh."

"Yes, Father, I promise." He sniffled and wiped a tear off his face.

"And I want you to keep up on your lessons. You need yo' education if you want to succeed in life. Learnin' is gettin' mo' and mo' impo'tant. Pretty soon it's going to be necessary!"

"Yes, Father, I'll get good grades, you'll see! I'll save all my work for you to see when you get back! I'll make you proud! I will!"

"Good boy!" He tousled his son's hair, as was his custom. Then he turned to his sobbing daughter. "Lizzy, please be brave. Can you do that fo' Daddy?"

She blew her nose into her handkerchief. "I'll try, Daddy." She looked so deeply into her father's eyes that she seemed to touch his soul. "I'm gonna miss you, Daddy." She wrapped his arms around him and squeezed with all her might!

"Me too, Lizzy. So much so." He held his daughter as tightly as he could, for as long as he could.

"We must go now." Maggie Mae's heart broke for her children, but they had to get to the train station. He was to report to Charleston, South Carolina, and the train ride was going to be quite long.

He hugged both his children one last time and climbed into the carriage. All the slaves were out front waving their master goodbye, with their bright white handkerchiefs, their cheeks glistening with tears.

The carriage ride was many miles. Normally, the trip into town was bumpy, and seemed to take hours. This trip seemed to be over in minutes, and later, she wouldn't recall feeling any bumps in the road. They exchanged few words on the way to Valdosta. Maggie Mae spent most of the trip with her head resting on Roland's strong shoulder. *How I'm going to miss this shoulder! My Lord, please bring my husband home safe and sound. In Jesus' name I pray. Amen.*

She wrapped herself around his arms. Her eyes were moist for the whole trip, and an occasional tear streamed down her face. She tried her best to conceal these, wiping them away when she thought that Roland wasn't looking. But he saw every single one.

As Roland held her hand, he immersed himself in his own thoughts. How was the plantation going to survive? He had made a promise to his father-in-law that he would take care of Maggie Mae, the children, and Magnolia Blossom Plantation. He said a silent prayer, addressing Maggie's father. "Pop, I promised you that I would take care of your little girl and the plantation. I must put that on hold and do my civic duty. With God's help, this confounded war will end very soon, and I'll return to take care of my one true love."

Way too soon, the carriage arrived in Valdosta.

"Are you certain you want to accompany me to the reporting station?"

"Yes, darlin', I'm sure. I want to spend as much time with you as I can." She again placed her head against his shoulder. "I'm truly afraid, Roland, I truly am."

He gently caressed his wife's face and kissed her forehead, very lightly. His heart ached at the thought of not being able to touch her porcelain white skin, caress her silky charcoal hair, kiss her plump, sensuous lips, or look into those sky-blue eyes. "Now, Maggie, we talked about this and we came to an agreement that you wouldn't worry."

In reality, he was very fearful as well, especially after learning the death toll during the latest battle. It was far beyond what he had expected. He feared for his life but didn't dare mention any of this to his wife. He was the man of the family and he had to stay strong for all of them, especially for Maggie Mae.

"I know, I know but…"

He placed his index finger over her mouth. "Please, no more, I beg of you. Let's just enjoy the brief time we have remaining."

They remained in each other's embrace for the remaining trip to Charleston. Maggie Mae could see the countryside moving past, through the window of the coach. With the clickety-clack of the wheels, combined with the gentle swaying of the coach and the strength of her man in her arms, her eyelids became heavier, and she dozed off to sleep. Roland, though, was too pumped up to sleep. He kept thinking of Maggie Mae running Magnolia Blossom Plantation alone—without his guidance. But he also knew that she had the help of Charles, the eldest of the slaves—er, workers, who was the informal leader. He always had been a tremendous help, since even before Roland had arrived on the scene. The sounds of distant gunshots punctuated the reality that was to be his very, very soon. A reality that, frankly, he dreaded.

Maggie Mae felt the cadence of the wheels begin to slow, as the train approached the station at Charleston. The brakes squealed, and she felt her body thrust forward in her seat as the train arrived at Charleston Station. It was late afternoon when they stepped off the train onto the noisy, crowded platform. It looked like an invasion of the station, although not by tourists. Many were there to enlist into the Army of the Confederate States of America. Just like Maggie Mae and Roland, dozens of couples held onto each other, as if for dear life. The fear and apprehension were palpable in the air and showed on their faces. Several women stood wiping tears from their faces, having already parted ways with their better halves, slowly boarding the train to return to their homes. How would they all face life without their man in charge? Other women, who looked much too old to have husbands enlisting, must have said good-bye to their young sons—not knowing if they'd ever return home. Maggie Mae's heart broke as she watched one woman embrace her son, then leave the platform in tears. They were on the same journey in life, and like these women, within an hour or so she, too, would be saying good-bye to Roland with no promise of tomorrow. She wore a brave face for Roland's sake.

Roland pulled out his letter and pointed to the exit. "This way, Dear." He gently guided his bride—after fourteen years of marriage, he still thought of her as his bride—toward the station, then through the exit onto the street, where many horse and carriage drivers waited for their passengers. Roland waved at one of them. "Good man, can you take us to the registration office?"

"Yes, suh," came a rather high-pitched voice. The driver seemed somewhat younger than Roland but was much more weathered and ragged. Driving a carriage all day, every day, took its toll, the couple thought. He dressed less smartly than they might have imagined, but he seemed to be rather fit—not particularly muscular, but moderately-built, from hefting folks' luggage all day. The driver quickly whisked up Roland's bag and placed it in the rear of the carriage while Roland helped his wife up and in. As she made herself comfortable, Roland looked around from the open-air carriage.

"I say, driver, how long will this ride take?"

"Ain't too far, I s'pose." He lifted the reins and snapped them. "Git up!" he cried as the horses pulled forward, and they were off.

"I do declare, he's about as useless as tits on a boar hog."

"Now, Roland, temper."

"Well, darlin', I can't be late. It's the govm'nt. Can't fool around with them."

"I understand, I do, but let the man do his job. Sit still and enjoy the ride." She winked and patted the empty seat next to her.

Roland didn't need to be told twice. He slid over to his wife's side and embraced her. She removed her bonnet and rested her head on his chest. His heart was beating quite quickly, and that calmed her nerves. She too, was apprehensive about his leaving to fight, but she had to be strong for both of them. "There now, isn't that better?"

"Oh yes, my darlin'. You have a way with me. Whatever will I do without you?"

She became somber. "I don't know, my love. I suppose you can write me every day. Will you promise me?"

"Of course, I promise. You'll get a letter from me every day."

She felt better. She closed her eyes and took in his fragrance of musk, imported cigars, and barber tonic. "Mmmmm, I'm gonna miss you, my darling."

"I'll miss you more." He turned his wife's face toward his and kissed her passionately. He did not want to let her go. He wanted to hold her in his arms forever. His body ached already, and she was still by his side.

"Whoa!" the driver yelled at the horses as they quickly came to a halt. "Army office," he announced as he jumped down to open the coach door. He fetched Roland's suitcase and placed it at the curb.

"Thank you, my good man." He gave the driver a quarter and helped his wife out onto the sidewalk.

"Very generous, sir. Much obliged!" He bowed and climbed back on the coach. Again, he snapped the reins and the horses galloped off.

"Well, here we are," Roland said with a tone of sorrow.

"Oh, Roland, can't you just tell them that you're a family man? And that you have a plantation to take care of? I'm sure they'll have pity on you and let you return home with me." Tears streamed down her rosy cheeks.

He could not bear to see her like this. He wanted to run back home with her, but he couldn't. He had to stay and register. But he hugged her tightly to hide his foggy eyes. He pulled his handkerchief out of his front jacket pocket and dried his eyes. "Here, my darling, allow me to dry your eyes. There is nothing I can do. Please have pity on your husband! I am already feeling very guilty about leaving you with the plantation and the slaves--"

"Workers, Roland, workers."

"Yes, I'm sorry, yes, workers." He paused. He was never going to get used to calling the slaves *workers*. That was something that his father-in-law was hellbent on instilling in him. He commended him for being a very generous man, but Roland had been raised quite differently. At the Moon plantation, they had been referred to as negros, and that's just how it was. It took him an awfully long time to think of them as workers. Workers were paid and slaves were owned. "Still a very heavy responsibility."

Maggie dried her eyes and recomposed herself. "Oh, don't you fret. We'll be fine, I assure you." She lied.

Roland rolled his eyes as he led his wife into the building. It was a large room, with perhaps a hundred men, many of them Confederate army officers, not to mention women and a smattering of children, all milling about. The walls were thick wooden boards badly in need of a coat of paint. The room smelled musty with a mixture of smoke from both cheap and expensive cigars. A permanent haze lingered in the air. The wood floor echoed with the sound of boots trampling around. "Well, I declare. They're runnin' all over hell's half acre in here." Roland just stared, blankly, saying nothing. He walked over to a table with a sign displaying "L through M." A young officer sat behind the table. He was a young lad, with golden hair. He wore a uniform that looked like it was made for someone much larger than he. While most of the men sported facial hair of one style or another, he had smooth skin, like a baby's bottom. Maggie Mae wondered whether this youngster was even old enough to shave. One thing was for sure: the boy had no personality. But then, a registrar didn't really need any sort of personality, did he?

"Name?" the young officer demanded, with a scowl.

"Roland David Moon."

"Date of birth?"

"June twenty-second, 1828."

"Sign here." He pointed at the line that asked for a signature.

Roland signed, and the young officer began to prepare his file. Once done, he turned and went through some clothes neatly folded on the floor, picked some articles out. He thrust the pile toward Roland. He wondered how such a young child had become his superior. "Here," the youngster said in a voice with no inflection. "Go over there for your checkup." He cocked his head toward a line of fearful and quivering young men, each holding his own pile of clothes.

Alongside them were either their mothers or their wives. When Roland tried to look into their eyes, he saw fear. He saw sadness. He saw the faintest of hearts. Suddenly, one of the recruits took off like a shot, running toward the door. In an instant, several burly officers ran over to the young man, with absolute terror in his eyes. His terror was compounded when he came face to face with several pistols.

"Oh, Roland, this is awful! Why, these soldiers are just out of childhood! Look at those faces." She pulled out her fan to cool herself. "And look at the women." She turned and looked around. "Well, as soon as I find the commander in charge of this abomination, I'll be bendin' his ear!" She closed her fan, slid it inside her sleeve, and marched toward what seemed like the commanding officer.

"Wait!" Roland tried to stop his wife from making a fool of herself, but when she was that determined, there was nothing he could say or do to stop her. He'd been down that road before. He liked that about her. In fact, it was one of the traits that attracted him to Maggie Mae. She was hot-tempered, and he loved the way she looked when she was angry—that is, when the anger wasn't directed at him. He slid the pile of clothes over to hide his arousal and stayed in that position until Maggie Mae had her say.

"Excuse me, sir." Maggie Mae stopped in front of the officer she had eyed seconds before, towering over her by a foot, at least.

"Ma'am." He tipped his hat and bowed to her.

"Are you in charge?" She looked him straight in the eyes.

"Yes, Ma'am. Brigadier General Sonders, at your service."

"Well, kind sir, you best dismiss all those boys over there." She pointed at the line where her husband stood.

Captivated by her extraordinary beauty, he decided to humor her. "And why would I do that?"

"Can't you see? They are barely out of childhood. You simply cannot have children fightin' for ya. That's outrageous!"

"Ma'am I do appreciate your concern, but I assure you, those 'boys' as you call them are all over seventeen years old." He crossed his arms over his chest.

"Seventeen!" She stepped back and wagged her finger at him. "That is no age for fightin'! Seventeen! They still need their mamas. I, as a mother, will not stand for this! May I speak to your superior, please?"

As much as she amused him, she was starting to create havoc and he would not have it. He looked over at Roland, who was looking the other way, obviously embarrassed by the behavior of his woman. "Ma'am, there is nobody here that is above me. Now, please, return to your husband's side while you still can." He didn't budge, but pointed her toward Roland. Her unwavering look and the fear behind it forced a change of heart. "Ma'am, believe me, I don't like this either, but I do not have a choice in the matter. I hope you understand."

As much as he agreed with her, he did not have any authority to let these young boys go home. He would be up on charges if he did.

With her head held high, Maggie Mae turned on her heels and returned to Roland's side. "Well, that was a waste of time."

Roland truly adored his wife, and her determination made her even more attractive. Her spunk was alluring. "Darling wife, you did the best you could."

"But they're so young…"

"I know, honey, I know." He wrapped his arm around her shoulders and pulled her closer. "You did the best you could." He lightly kissed her cheek.

"I'm just so troubled. I feel useless."

As they approached the medical section, another exceptionally young soldier, sitting at a desk, asked, "Name and date of birth."

"Roland David Moon, June twenty-second, 1828."

The young soldier made a mark in the notebook. "That way." He commanded again. "Ma'am, you can have a seat over there." He pointed to a row of chairs occupied by the mothers that were standing alongside their sons. There were a few young brides, but she was the only oldest wife there.

She sat in the last chair next to the window. Nervously, she removed her gloves and placed them gently on her lap. She untied her bonnet and placed it on her lap. Then she just sat there looking out the window at a large Magnolia that was in blossom. It reminded her of the plantation. The tree was so compelling that everyone who lived on the plantation would stop and simply stare at it when it was in bloom. It was also the reason her parents had named her Magnolia.

What am I to do when Roland is gone? The plantation will be all mine to manage. She knew her workers would take good care of it while he was at war, but she still worried. With her head leaning against the windowpane, her eyelids became very heavy....

It was a bright, sunny day and the rays shimmered on the backs of the workers. Everyone around was busy working, picking the cotton while singing a familiar tune with angelic voices. The young children were drumming to the beat as they joined in the song:

Oh Lordy, pick a bale o' cotton
Oh Lordy, pick a bale a day
Oh Lordy, pick a bale o' cotton
Oh Lordy, pick a bale a day
Gonna jump down, turn around
Pick a bale o' cotton
Gonna jump down, turn around

Pick a bale a day…

"*La, la, la, la, pick a bale o' cotton...*"

"*La, la, la, la...*"

"*La, la, la...*"

"*Darlin', darlin'...*"

"*La, la...*"

"Darlin', Maggie Mae."

She felt a hand on her shoulder.

"Darlin', Maggie Mae?"

She startled. "Oh! My, I must have dozed off."

He thought she was the most beautiful creature when she slept peacefully. "That's quite all right, darlin'."

She looked up at him. "Well, look at you, all handsome in your uniform." She smiled. She had never seen her husband in uniform before. It made her feel odd. Like a wanting. Like a desire. Like a tingle between her legs.

"Why thank ya!" He pushed his pectorals out and placed his fists on his hip.

"How long do we have before you go?"

"About an hour or so, I reckon."

"Well, all right then. Come along." She hooked her arm into his and gently pulled him toward the entrance.

"Where are we going?"

"To take a photograph."

Chapter Four

A bright sunbeam pierced the bedroom and landed squarely on Maggie Mae's face. She pulled her pillow over herself to shield her face. Still groggy, she slid her hand over to Roland's side of the bed. She felt the empty pillow and sat bolt upright, remembering that he wasn't there. "Oh, yeah," She silently whispered. "He's gone." She blinked a few times to focus, then got up and opened the curtains to let the sunshine flow in. *What a glorious day. I wonder what my Roland is doing.* Today was exactly one month since he'd left for his military duty. She went to her bedside to look at the photograph that they had taken the day he left. Roland was so handsome and proud while standing and wearing his Confederate uniform. She looked like royalty seated next to him. He was holding her hand as he looked into the camera with a serious look on his face. She knew he was worried about leaving the plantation in the care of only his wife and the workers. She picked up the frame and ran her fingers over her husband's face as tears began to stream down hers.

"Why did you have to leave?" she pressed the frame against her heart. "I miss you so!" She heard a light knock on her door.

"Come in Flora."

Flora pushed the heavy door open and began to pull pieces of clothing from the armoire.

"That's some nice photograph, Maggie." She placed the garments on the bed.

"Yes. We were happy that day, even though we knew we were going to be apart for a long time."

"Oh, don't fret, Maggie, it'll pass quickly. You'll see."

"Well, I don't know…it's been a month already, but it seems like a year."

Flora couldn't argue that point as she felt the same way.

"He promised me he would write every day but all I've received is one letter!" she pulled his letter out of her nightstand and waved it in the air angrily.

"Now, Maggie, as your friend, I must tell ya to pull yo'self togethuh. We all need you here. To guide us and tell us what to do. Now, hurry up and let's git you dressed."

At eight o'clock sharp, she was in the dining room being served breakfast, and shortly after her two children joined her.

"What are we learning today Mama?" Lizzy asked excitedly.

During the war, Maggie Mae and Roland decided not to send the children to the schoolhouse in town, as they had heard rumors that the Yankees were going to the schoolhouses and taking the older boys to serve in the Union Army.

Roland would say, "There is no way in hell that my children will be serving the North! No sir-ree!"

Maggie Mae was in complete agreement and took it upon herself to homeschool Lizzie and Pauly. It was nearly impossible to obtain any sort of textbook, so she had to make do. She knew that her children needed the basics: Readin', Writin', and 'Rithmetic. She was able to teach 'Rithmetic from her knowledge, but the Readin' and Writin' was a horse of a different color. She had some books of the Classics on the bookshelf, and of course, the Holy Bible. She would have the children read Bible passages, and then explain them to her. She also would have them transcribe Bible passages onto paper, and also would assign them essays and book reports based on the Classics. She previously had taught Flora to read and write and to do numbers, so she assisted Maggie Mae in teaching the children.

One beautiful sunny morning, Maggie Mae announced, "Well, I'm not in the mood for teachin' today, so how about we do some learnin' outdoors?"

"Yes, Mama, I'd like that," Lizzy cried out.

"Me as well, Mama!" Pauly cried out just like his big sister. He always tried to match what she was doing or saying.

"Well, all right then. Finish your breakfast."

They set off on a beautiful February morning. There was not a cloud in the sky and birds were singing a tune of early spring. Maggie Mae was carrying a picnic basket filled with goodies prepared by Chesney. As they walked into the woods, Maggie Mae asked her children the names of all the trees, shrubs, and plants they encountered, and when they were graced by the presence of a resident animal, she promptly asked them what they were called and which animal family they belonged to. She made a mental note of all the correctly answered questions, as she would need to register them in the notebook she kept. A couple hours later, when they reached the creek, Lizzy opened the blanket and set it on the grass.

"Finally! I'm famished!" Pauly exclaimed.

"Boy, you are growin' too quickly! No wonder you're always hungry." She gently caressed her son's face. He was a nearly identical copy of his mother: the same curly black hair, sapphire eyes, and fair skin—except for his manly features. Oh, yes. He was going to steal the hearts of all the young belles one day!

"Now tell me, Lizzy, what would you like to do for your birthday?"

Elizabeth Anita Moon would be fourteen in March. She was the spitting image of her father, with the same reddish hair, freckled complexion, and sky-blue eyes. She had much of that rebellious Irish blood in her, too. This concerned Maggie Mae, especially now that Lizzie was becoming a young lady. and without Roland present, Maggie Mae was afraid that she wouldn't be able to handle her.

"I don't know, Mama. I'll have to think about it."

"Just think. Two more years, and you'll be formally introduced into society."

"Does that mean I'll have to marry?"

"Why yes. That is the tradition, yes."

"Well, I don't want to marry. I want to enjoy my life while I can." She pouted.

"Why, Elizabeth Anita, you must marry! If you wait too long, your contenders will pick other young ladies and you'll become an old maid. Is that what you want?" she peered at her.

"Well, no…I do want to marry eventually, just not at sixteen, is all."

"I see." She paused to collect her thoughts. "When I met your daddy, we didn't marry right away. We waited. But I did promise I would marry him. There's no reason why you can't do that as well. What do you think?"

Lizzy's eyes brightened up. "Yes, Mama, I'd like that. We can stay engaged for a while. I wanna make sure I really love him."

"Yes, darlin', I understand."

"Mama, how did you know?" Lizzy asked with inquiring eyes.

"Well, I can't explain it. You just know, I reckon. Perhaps it was the way he looked at me from across the room. Or the spark I felt when he took me in his arms as we danced. Or the shiver down my spine when he kissed my hand." She sighed. "You just know, I suppose."

"Oh, how romantic."

Maggie Mae smiled and looked around for Pauly. When she couldn't see him, she became worried. "Pauly, where are you?" no answer. "Pauly?" she shouted as she got up to begin searching for him. "Lizzy, go look over there and I'll go this way but come back here, ya hear?"

"Yes, Mama." She took off following the creek.

Maggie Mae scurried the opposite way calling her son as loud as she could. Then she heard horses. She looked straight up the creek and saw an infantry. "Maybe they've seen him." As she approached, she saw what seemed to be their leader, and she stopped to recompose herself.

"Good afternoon Ma'am, Brigadier General James P. Anderson, at your service." He announced as he tipped his hat. The general was an imposing figure, sitting tall in the saddle. Although dusty from being on the trail, she could tell his boots had recently been shined. His trousers had lost their sharp crease from being in the field for so long. His jacket showed the wear that months of war leaves. His beard was well-combed, and his face washed. Maggie, like most women, felt an attraction to the man in uniform.

"Good afternoon." She curtsied. "My name is Mrs. Magnolia Moon and I'm looking for my son, Roland. Have you seen him?"

"You mean that young man over there?" he pointed to one of his men who had the boy riding behind him on his horse.

"Roland Paul Moon! How dare you wander off like that! You come down here so I can knock you into the middle of next week!"

This lady has a lot of zeal! I really love a quick-tempered woman. "Now, Ma'am, don't be so harsh on him. This here is a future Confederate soldier, he is."

Maggie Mae was taken aback from the general's comment and her porcelain white face lit up like a firecracker. "Soldier? Oh, but he's only eleven years old. He's way too young for fightin'!" she went and pulled her son down off the horse. "Now, come along Pauly." She grabbed his hand and pulled him away from the group.

"But Mama, I wanna stay. Please let me stay and ride with them!" He looked up at his mother, his blue eyes glistening.

"Now, son, you best listen to your mama. We can't take you until you're sixteen, ya' hear?"

Pauly crouched in disappointment. "Yes, sir."

"What did I show you, when you address an officer, young man?"

Roland snapped to attention, his left arm at his side, and his right hand coming up to the outside corner of his eye, in a sharp salute.

The general quickly returned the salute and said, "As you were, soldier."

Pauly's right arm went back to his side. He beamed with pride at the attention the general paid him.

Maggie Mae watched as the soldiers slowly trotted off. She was thankful to the general for talking some sense into her son. Just the thought of being without her husband ***and*** her son made her stomach turn a somersault. *No son of mine will be fightin' for slavery, that's for certain!* They walked in silence back to the spot where the blanket was. There, waiting for them, was Lizzy.

"Mama! Where did you find him?"

Maggie pulled her son's ear as they approached the girl. She was fuming.

"Ow!!"

"Why, he was riding with the cavalry, he was!"

"Yeah, it was fun! And I'm gonna join when I'm sixteen."

"Oh, no you're not! I will not permit it! No son of mine will fight and probably lose his life over slavery of the negro." She forced him to sit. "Now, you listen to me. Those slaves, as the Confederates call them, are human beings, just like you and me. Ya hear? You and your sister were brought up like I was, respectin' and treatin' them as our friends and family."

"But Mama…"

"Don't 'but Mama' me! Don't you be interruptin' when I speak." She took a deep breath as she gently brushed her son's hair away from his face. "Do you want to fight in a war that forces you to be enemies with Jupiter? Or Lewis? Or Harry? Or Franky? Because that's what they're gonna teach ya. Do you understand son?"

"I suppose."

"They're gonna teach you that negros have half the brains that the white folk do. Just think of how smart your negro friends are. Why, some of them are as smart as whips, they are. So, let me ask ya, do you agree with the Confederates?"

Pauly thought of the many times his negro friends helped him with his lessons. They got his tit out of a ringer many times so they could all play together or go fishing. He looked at his mother's flushed face and hung his head in shame. "No, Mama, I do not."

"Well good. You've come to your senses. That's my boy." She gave her son a loud kiss on his cheek. "Your daddy would be so proud of you right now."

"Ummm…then how come daddy is fightin' in the war? Does he agree with the Confederates?"

He did have a point. "Well, darlin', he had to go because he was summoned."

"Summoned?"

"Yes, son, it means he was forced to enlist. He had no choice because he was drafted. When you're drafted, you must go; otherwise they'll arrest you and put you in jail."

"So, when I turn sixteen, I will receive a summoned?"

"Summons, dear." The fear of her son being drafted to fight this awful war terrified her. She pressed her son's black, curly head of hair against her heart. "I certainly hope not. I pray that this war will be over by the time you turn sixteen. I wouldn't be able to stand you walking out on your mama and fightin' a war that just ain't right." She rocked him and prayed: *Oh, Lord, please don't let my baby go to this terrible war, I beg of you!*

Around three they collected their belongings and began the walk back to the plantation. Mother and children discussed more of the war and of slavery. "Let me tell you a story. It's about Jonas."

"Yes, Mama," the children replied.

"Well, one time, when Jonas was just about your age, Pauly, a nearby plantation owner accused him of stealing a baby hog. A lynch mob came to the Magnolia Blossom Plantation with the intention of hoisting Jonas up in the nearest tree. But Grandpa Terry refused to hand him over, because he believed that his slave was not lying.

George demanded a fair trial for Jonas, but the mob wasn't hearing of it. Then Grandpa went with his 'workers,' pulled all the guns out of the armory, and waited for the mob to return. When they arrived, they were all staring down the barrels of fifty-seven guns, all locked and loaded, ready to shoot. All the pitchforks and shovels in the world couldn't handle that number of blazing guns, so they grumbled a bit and went home. Nobody got hurt that day, and after some investigating, they learned that the son of the neighboring plantation owner—a white boy, had stolen the little piglet to sell it for money. He didn't even get a slap on the hand, but the mob was ready to kill an innocent negro boy just because someone thought they saw him in the vicinity of the pig sty. After that incident, Grandpa never came to any conclusions about anybody, until there was a fair trial."

"That was some story Mama."

"Indeed, it was. Your grand-daddy was a very fair man."

"I miss him, Mama."

"Me too, said Lizzy"

"Yes, I miss him too, my children. So very much."

Chapter Five

It was a bright and warm day on April sixth and the reveille was sounded late to allow the weary soldiers a day of rest.

There were many fires blazing around the camp as the men idled around them. Some preparing breakfast, others writing love letters to their beloved, the younger soldiers writing to their mothers and some just carelessly inspecting their limbs and paraphernalia.

Roland, who was now a Captain, was one of the many who were writing to their wives or betrothed. His pencil was short and stubby due to the many times it had been sharpened roughly for the lead to appear. By now, his feet were so blistered due to his boots having their soles worn out, that he limped and with every limp he agonized and distressed with pain.

Many of the frowsy-headed officers occasionally peered, languidly calling to their negro servants to fetch water, dust a coat or polish a scabbard. Many trim young mounted orderlies, bearing dispatches that were obviously important swiftly moved amongst the momentarily relaxed men and unmounting when they arrived at their destination.

Roland's group had arrived late in the evening and situated less than a mile from the Union camp. The order was to remain all night lying on their weapons. Thankfully, the cool nocturn air made it less insufferable.

It wasn't even dawn when they were on their feet and ordered forward in the line of battle. There was a feeling of a tug of war as the brigade had received a sharp word of command. They all sprung to their feet, even the negros. They all felt the ground trembling and the sound of grumblings in the distance similar to the growling of many of men's stomachs. All the Officers appeared and quickly gathered in groups as Headquarters became a swarming hive.

The rebels were very anxious to play this new battle that had been ordered but then realized the storm of conflict was in the rush. The line of battle was several miles long and the section of the line where Roland was commanding, advanced was over an undulating wooded country. The line marched in perfect order and on the right and left as far as the eye could see, the line of battle and the regimental battle flags were waving in the calm morning breeze.

They received orders to advance until they landed upon an elevation and looking down the decline some four hundred yards, there stood a Union line of battle.

"Hold your fire!" was heard by all ears while they advanced to be within two hundred yards of the Union line. As soon as they were close enough, the Union weapons began to shoot and the Rebels didn't hesitate to respond.

"Everyone git down!" another order was heard and all obeyed as they evacuated their weapons. Then a silent order arrived to get up quickly and charge but the charge was far from silent. The Rebels began to shoot as they yelled at the top of their lungs as the Union soldiers took to their heels. Afterwards, that yell was named the "Rebel Yell".

The Rebels ran into an artillery camp and as an evidence that they had taken the Union soldiers by complete surprise, they found breakfast still cooking on their campfires, camp equipage, clothing, blankets, ammunition, rifles, glass, silverware and an endless variety of foods like pickled fruit and vegetables.

Roland immediately went to the boots storage and looked for a decent pair of boots. He quickly found a pair that looked like his size. He swiftly removed his and grabbed a pair of heavy wool socks. As he slid up the socks, trying not to move the bandage that surrounded his blisters, he slid his feet into the boots.

"Oh, my, they feel good." He stomped his feet on the ground as a gesture of victory with his hands proudly placed on his hips. He felt like a strong man again. Then he joined his brigade who were eating the remnants of the cooked food. He wondered how the Union army was so stocked up while the Rebels were running dangerously low on supplies. "Damn Yanks!" and shoved another big bite into his mouth.

While the Rebels were enjoying the free supplies, the Union soldiers were re-grouping over the hill and opened fire on them. Having the advantage of the first fire, Brigadier General Gladden was mortally wounded by the first volley as well as a number of other officers and men. The General was in the rear of the regiment when he was wounded and was carried to the tent where the wounded soldiers were. His leg was amputated and the shrill of pain was heard throughout the camp. He died shortly after that.

Colonel Zach Deas, who was the Senior Colonel of the brigade, took command. After a moment of silence was given to pay their respects to the fallen General, Colonel Deas began to bark orders.

The men reformed at the Union camp and were ordered to move forward upon the enemy. They soon repulsed them a second time and during that long, bloody day, they repeatedly charged and counter charged. The rush of the storm of battle seemed to make the ground beneath them tremble.

A fellow Captain, Charles Waddell, who was from Texas had become good friends with Roland. They were about the same age and they were both married with two children a piece. Chucky would go on and on about his beloved Claire meanwhile, Roland did the same with his Maggie Mae. It was clear that they had become dear friends in the midst of this tragic war. They both couldn't wait to return to their beloved families and vowed to write each other often whenever the day came that the bloody war ended. Chucky had brought his own rifle to battle that was bought out west and it was made out of fine materials. He insisted to use it when he shot and killed the Yankee soldiers. He shot many a soldier but on that day, when he was on his knees re-loading his rifle, a Union bullet struck him in the heel, which disabled him. Roland immediately barked his men to take him to the tent but when the doctors told him he would need to be amputated, he refused.

"Now, Chucky, you've got to do as they tell you. Don't ya want ta shoot them Yanks?" Roland's voice was frantic as he desperately wanted his new friend to listen to him.

"No, my friend, I'm gonna take what the Lord is givin' me." Clutching his rifle, he handed it to Roland. "Here, you shoot them bastards now."

"I…I…" he choked up.

"Now listen, I want you to write to my precious Claire, yo' heah? I want her to git a letter from my friend, not the gov'mint. Can you promise me that?"

Roland was unable to speak. He only nodded.

"Good man."

Roland stood by his side until he took his last breath. Then he slowly closed his eyes and covered him with the bloody sheet. He took the rifle, polished as much blood as he could off of it and headed to the position where his regiment was. He passed many a dead body on his way there; many with their eyes still open, some already being pecked at by the bloodthirsty ravens. He even heard some moaning and sighing but he couldn't stop to help, rather he silently prayed that the good Lord would take their souls up into heaven for that is where these men belonged.

"Oh, those cursed guns!" Roland thought as he took his position inside the Hornet's Nest; a name given to the area of the Shiloh battlefield where both side repeatedly attacked each other. The bullets sounded like angry hornets and many commented that it was like a hornet's nest in there.

Although it was long enough to be the key in holding back the Rebels onslaught, it was also long enough for Grant to organize a defense and receive reinforcements. The narrow farm road ambles generally southeast from its junction with the Eastern Corinth Road, fairly level toward its northwest end and it was a sharp climb up a hill in the center. Wallace and Prentiss lumped their soldiers together in the Hornet's Nest, confusing matters. The true defense strength of the Hornet's Nest lay in the fact that in order to attack Confederates, the Yankees had to charge uphill through obstructions of blackberry bushes and undergrowth, making it impossible for the Yankees to maintain their formations.

As dawn broke, on the morning of April sixth, the Union soldiers were some 5400 men and by midmorning, the Confederates had emerged from the woods to begin their attack in earnest, after initially being slowed by skirmishers.

"They are like a Kansas tornado!" cried one of the Union commanders as many Yankees were captured or killed.

The Yankees managed to repulse a series of Confederate charges throughout the day with exploding artillery rounds and sparks falling from the flames of shooting out of the muzzles of muskets which caused the woods to catch fire. This caused many Confederates to be burned to death. By four in the afternoon, the Confederates commanders assembled the largest grand battery of artillery ever seen on the North American continent and the short and shells were hurled into the areas of the Sunken Road and inside the Hornet's Nest.

Wallace was mortally wounded and left for dead on the field. Prentiss was captured—which allowed him to later write the accounts of what happened. He, of course, emphasized the defense of the Hornet's Nest as the key to holding back the Rebel tide long enough for Grant to organize a defensive line on the bluffs above Pittsburgh Landing. Prentiss' would live on to tell the story about the Hornet's Nest and would be one of the chosen historians to tell the tale of the Shiloh battlefield. Nobody ever really knew the exact truth about the Hornet's Nest but based in part on the number of bodies found on the right and left sides of the battlefield, as compared to the smaller number in the center where the Hornet's Nest lay, his story was most probably a truthful one.

Roland was barking orders to his men as he followed the orders sent to him by Brigadier General Daniel Ruggles. At first, he was surprised how much power the Confederates gained but by the end of the afternoon, the casualties that happened elsewhere on the field, signaled the end for the Hornet's Nest defenders.

At one point, while Roland was helping one of his younger soldiers, he felt a sudden pain in his left side.

"Come men! Let's get him to the tent!" he ordered.

Four of his men whipped their rifles over their shoulders and lifted the injured man by one of his limbs.

"Am I gonna die?" the young man asked, barely out of adulthood.

Although it looked horribly bad, he said: "No, son, you're not gonna die, you're goin' home."

"What's your name son?"

"Paul, sir, like Saint Paul."

"Paul, that's my son's name." he smiled at the young man as he recollected looking into his son's eyes as he left that bitter day.

As they placed the young soldier on one of the injury beds, he grabbed onto Roland's arm. "Please don't leave me, please?" he pleaded.

"I won't son. I'm not goin' anywhere. I promise." He was trying to hold his tears back but the sting of salt and blood was felt.

"Sir, how're we doin'?" he mumbled.

"We're winnin', son, winnin'! We're teachin' them Yanks a thing or two 'bout fightin'." While he kept his right hand on the dying man's chest, he touched his left side and without bringing his hand up too high, he saw a left hand covered in blood. He winced but didn't say a word. He kept his focus on Paul as he wiped his hand clean on his trousers.

Paul slowly pulled a letter out of his front pocket. "Please, sir, can ya give this to my mama?"

Roland took it and looked at the return address. It was from Marianna, Florida. "Yes, I will, I promise." Just like he did with his friend, he made the same promise to Paul. He folded it and held it between his right hand and Paul's chest. He felt no movement in his chest area and when he looked at his face, he was smiling.

"You're smilin'. Maybe you've seen our Lord." He closed his eyes and left the letter on Paul's chest knowing well that the burial crew would collect his things and mail them to his mother.

Finally, Federal commanders were giving away after hours of intense fighting.

As darkness fell upon the bloody field, both sides disengaged for the night. Roland did as the others. With rifle in hand, he sat leaning against a Magnolia tree and fell asleep.

As soon as the sun shone its rays warming the hell bound field, the Union suddenly had quadrupled of size. The ease of their victory against the Confederates was surprising. The majority of the Confederates were tired, weakened, injured, dying or dead.

The bloody battle of Shiloh left nearly 24000 dead, wounded or missing and made the entire nation realize that the Civil War was not going to end quickly nor would it end without the high price of human lives.

Chapter Six

April 8, 1862

My dearest Maggie,

I received your letter yesterday. I must say, it really boosted my morale to hear from you! My God, Maggie, I miss you so! I miss Magnolia Blossom Plantation! I miss our workers! (I think I'm finally getting used to calling them workers!)

War is hell! It's a miserable, dirty, nasty affair. There's nothing glamorous about it. I'll spare you the sordid details. Suffice it to say that as soon as I can get out of this Godforsaken situation and get back to my sweetheart, our children, and our plantation, I shall!

I hope that all is well with you. I know that you are taking care of things in my absence. You have a way to getting things done, and I rest well knowing that you're there. I trust that Will and Flora are assisting you with the workers.

Please give Lizzie and Pauly a big hug for me and tell them I love then and miss them a lot!

I love all of you with all of me!

All my love,

Roland

Maggie must have read that letter over and over, a thousand times! At least, that's how it seemed to her. And throughout the next few months, Roland's letters arrived more frequently. In those letters, he gave instructions to the workers, as well as writing phrases of love to his bride—along with compliments and recommendations to his children.

~~~~~~

Flora Jefferson and her husband Jonas lived in the closest negro quarters, about fifty feet away from the back of the main house. They had four sons: Jupiter who was twelve, Lewis age ten, Joseph, just barely eight, and Will Junior, the youngest at six. She also raised Maggie Mae's children.

Flora grew up on the plantation, the same as Maggie Mae, and they had been best friends growing up. Maggie Mae wanted only Flora to be her maid—no one else. The two women knew each other so well that they knew each other's thoughts. Sometimes Maggie Mae would say, "Flora, did you hear what I was thinkin'?" and Flora would promptly reply, "Yessum, you were thinkin' 'bout..." and she would complete the thought almost all the time. Sometimes, one of them would approach the other and start talking, as though answering a spoken question.

The only downside was that Flora would have to act like a real slave when white people were around. But Flora didn't mind, because the white people would eventually leave, and she could return being herself.

The next house over was occupied by Rose and Ned Steward. Rose was the dressmaker of the plantation. All Rose had to do was look at a picture of a dress and she could have it done in a week or two, depending on how complicated it was or how long the fabric took to arrive from New York or overseas. Rose even made clothes for the male children and the black adult males. It was the norm for the owners to go to a tailor for their clothes, no matter how good Rose may have been. Rose and Ned had six children, most of whom worked on the plantation, except for Molley, who was learning to weave, and little Will, who was only three years old.

Chesney and Cato Johnson lived in the third house along with their five children. Chesney was the cook of the plantation, and Cato, who had a limp from a bad beating he had taken from his previous slaveowner, helped her with the food preparation and vegetable gardening. Their three sons worked on the plantation and their daughter, Janette, was learning to cook. She would be taking over for her mother one day.

The oldest slave family on the plantation were. Charles and Harriet Willis, the parents of Flora, Rose, Chesney, and Asher, their eldest. Asher married Fanny, who gave birth to only two children, Lily and Melton. She had been Anita Terry's personal maid, but after Anita passed, Fanny joined her in-laws in cleaning the main house and doing gardening. Their slave house was the largest of all, as they held seniority above the other three families.

Magnolia Blossom Plantation was a perfectly oiled machine. The Terrys had been firm believers that if you treated your slaves with compassion, understanding, and friendship, the Lord would reward you twofold, and that's exactly why the plantation was the most envied and sought-after estate in the all of Georgia. Even without the head of the household present, Magnolia Blossom was flourishing.

Every time Maggie Mae went into town, folks who wanted to buy the plantation continually approached her. She didn't understand why these offers that came her way all the time.

Until one afternoon, when Benjamin Hart approached. His last name was misleading. It most certainly did not reflect his inner character. He was the most evil, ruthless, and heartless man she had ever met. He was still angry with Maggie Mae for rejecting his son, James and instead, marrying Roland. He could not wait for his paybacks.

"Mrs. Moon, may I have a word, please?" He stopped her on her way out of the general store dressed in his normal arrogance and a green velvet suit.

"Good afternoon, Mr. Hart." She swiftly swirled around him and made her way to her carriage. "I'm dreadfully sorry, but I must be going. There is always so much work to do at the plantation, you know. Especially with my darling Roland gone."

"Please, Mrs. Moon, this will take only a few minutes." He sounded docile but his intentions were quite callous.

She rolled her eyes. She loathed that man. "Charles, please stay here. I'll be back before you know it."

"Yes, Missy Maggie." Charles held deep concern for his former master's daughter. She had always treated him like her uncle, and he held her in the upmost respect. He had promised her father, on his deathbed, that he would be the father she no longer had.

She painted a smile on her face. "Very well, Mr. Hart, but please make it quick. I have work to do and I really must be going."

He bowed and guided her toward the tea house, opening the door for her. He waited, as she made herself comfortable and removed her gloves and bonnet. Then, Benjamin cleared his throat. "Mrs. Moon, I'll get to the point. I am extremely interested in purchasing your plantation—along with your slaves, of course. I am ready to pay you a pretty penny for it."

"Mr. Hart, I am—"

"Please, Mrs. Moon, hear me out." He tried to be gentle, but his tone deceived him. "I know that without your husband around, God bless him for defending our Confederacy the way he is, you are strugglin' to manage the slaves, educate your children, and sell your crops. Keepin' face. I can only imagine what that's like, and I'd like to relieve you of this burden."

She wanted to yell at him, *"Burden? Burden? How dare you! You pompous ass!"* But her daddy had taught her well, not to fly off the handle. She bit her tongue.

"Sell it to me. I will pay you generously. Name your price."

Maggie Mae had to thoroughly think her response through. She wanted to tell him to shove his money where the sun don't shine, but that was not ladylike. She slowly slid one of her gloves on. "Mr. Hart, you most certainly are very generous, but even if I did want to sell the plantation to you, I legally cannot. My father left it to my husband, Roland." She stood as she slipped her second glove onto her hand and carefully placed her bonnet back on her head.

"How could that be? You are the rightful heir of that property, not Roland. That's preposterous." He was raising his voice.

"I'll have you know, Mr. Hart, that my father loved Roland like a son; hence, he decided to leave everything to him. And I could not agree more. You see, my daddy was a very wise man." She wore a gracious smile as she headed for the door. "Good day, Mr. Hart." She opened the door, leaving him standing there like a bump on a log.

He gritted his teeth so hard that his pulse throbbed in his cheeks. He simply tipped his hat and wished her a good day in return.

As soon as Charles saw Maggie coming, he opened the carriage door. She winked at him as she climbed inside. He shut the door and grinned. Even though he had not heard what transpired, he clearly saw Mr. Hart's reactions through the window. In his mind, he pieced together the most likely conversation. Then, he quickly climbed up on the driver seat and cracked the whip.

On the ride home, her thoughts drifted off to her husband, her soulmate, who had been gone much too long. She pulled a crumpled piece of paper out of her bag and carefully unfolded it. The ink was smeared from her tears and from the humidity.

My dearest Maggie Mae, it began. *I am doing well. But war truly is hell. I've said it before, and I still say it. We are fighting American vs. American. Never before have we been in this situation! I pray for a quick end to this insanity, and a return to American unity. We cannot exist as two separate countries. The North is industrial, and the South is agricultural. We complement each other. This disunity will be the death of this once great nation!*

My sweet Maggie, I promise to you that I will return as soon as God allows me to. I love you with all my heart and soul. I feel like half a person without you by my side. Like our nation, I feel lost when we are not together. You are my life and my very world. I have you on my mind continuously. It's what keeps me going, knowing that you and I will be reunited soon!

Please, keep our plantation safe from malefactors. Especially, do not allow that snake Benjamin Hart anywhere near the Plantation. He is as evil as the serpent that tricked Eve into eating the forbidden fruit.

I count the days until my eyes gaze on your countenance once more.

Your adoring husband,
Roland

Then a sly thought came to her mind. She couldn't wait for the carriage to pull up in front of the plantation house. When it finally did, she rushed inside and called, "Chesney!"

The cook came out like a shot, wiping her hands on her apron. "Yes, Missy?"

"I'm going to have a party! The biggest and best party this town has ever seen! We will show that arrogant man, his entire family, and the neighboring plantation owners just how well the Moons are doing!"

"Yes, missy? What do you want me to do?"

"I want you to look up those recipes of yours and put together a fabulous menu, ya hear?"

Chesney smiled from ear to ear. She loved to cook, and she especially loved to cook for guests. She hadn't done it in a long time, and an appropriate dinner party was way overdue. "Yes, yes! I'll start right away!" She turned on her heels and disappeared into the kitchen.

"Rose!"

Rose appeared from the sewing room. "Yes, Missy?"

"Look what I brought you." As Charles strode into the room holding a package, she stopped him, took the package, and unrolled the prettiest satin brocade fabric that had ever been seen in these parts.

"Oh, Missy, this is so pretty!" She slid her hand over the fuchsia fabric. "Do you have something in mind?"

"Oh, yes." With a grand smile, she handed Rose a catalog. "Here. Go to page four."

Rose sat on the chair and opened to page four. "Oh, Missy! This gown is stunnin'…an' I can see it on ya already." She whisked up a corner of the fabric and covered Maggie's front with it. "Yessum, I see it well."

"Tell me, Rose, how long will it take you?"

"Well, Missy Maggie, the roses are gonna be challengin' but I think I can have it ready in a couple of weeks."

"Good. I'll set the date then, and I'll give you a few extra days for good measure." She hugged Rose. "I'm so excited!"

Rose folded the fabric back up and, with the catalog tucked under her arm, headed back to the sewing room with a bounce in her step. There, her precious Grasshopper sewing machine was waiting for her to create her next masterpiece. She gently placed the roll of fabric on the armchair and sat down in the matching one to study the picture in the catalog.

The next two weeks were all about preparation. The house was methodically cleaned from top to bottom, every nook and cranny scrubbed. Every cup and dish was washed and dried; every knickknack was cleaned and polished; every painting was dusted; and each cobweb was swept away. Even the outdoor plants, flowers, and trees underwent trimming, weeding, watering, and seeding. The house and land were upgraded overall to look like a house belonging to the richest slave-owning family in the Confederacy. The large magnolia tree received a meticulous trimming, and the Spanish moss was removed from the oak trees—not completely, though. Enough was left to make the oaks look stately and majestic.

When the main house was finally clean to Maggie Mae's satisfaction, the stalls were tackled. They were washed down with soap and water on the outside, and each grain of muddled straw was replaced with thin, new straw. The horses were moved outdoors to the paddock and not let back into the stables until shortly before the party. Once the horses were settled in the stables, the paddock was also cleaned and the fence washed.

Even the negro quarters were scrubbed, inside and out. A fresh coat of paint made every house look brand new. The small front gardens and the roadway were freshened up with young greenery and gravel.

Finally, all their clothes were washed, dried, ironed, and restored back to their original shape. Maggie Mae gave each woman one of her mother's dresses as a gift, and Rose was given the task of fitting them to their new owners. The growing teen boys were given some of George's clothes, since there wasn't time to have Rose sew them new ones. The growing boys welcomed those old clothes, because they felt like responsible adults in them, and all the while keeping the memory of their deceased master alive.

On the 28th of May, 1862, Magnolia Blossom Plantation was ready for the most lavish party ever given. The food was set up on the dining room table. There was a vast variety of game, vegetables grown in the plantation garden, fruit that arrived in from all over the state, and an extravagant layout of pies, cakes, and pastries. A mixture of everything was set up on every table, small and large, that could be found. All the adult male workers dressed in the finest waiter attire, while the women were adorned with the finest cotton aprons and matching bonnets.

The older teenagers greeted the guests in front of the porch, assigned to parking the horses and carriages that arrived. They'd never had a chance to drive a horse and carriage until then, and they were hardly able to contain their excitement.

A small orchestra was set up in the anteroom and a small area had the rugs removed, so there would be a makeshift dance floor for anyone so inclined.

Lizzy and Pauly were mingling with the other older children brought by their parents. There were six white children in total, and Charles gave them strict instructions to stay in the library as not to cause any trouble.

Magnolia Mae was upstairs in her bedroom, perfecting her appearance. She put on her nicest necklace, made sure that every hair was in place, and checked to see that her brand new gown covered herself perfectly. Flora entered the room, laughing.

"What is it, Flora?" Maggie asked.

"Well, looks ta me like your presence iz desired—not as much by them women—but them men look like roosters in a room fulla hens."

"What are they sayin'?"

She opened the door just enough to allow some conversations to float into the room as Maggie Mae continued with her hair and put some color on her porcelain white face.

"I hear, 'Where is she? What's keepin' her? I wonder what she's wearin'?' " and much like that." She turned to her mistress. "Ready, Miss Maggie?"

"I am." She softly ran her palms over her new gown to smooth it, as she gracefully arose and headed for the open door.

"You is sumpin' purdy, you is!"

Maggie Mae simply nodded as she began to slowly and elegantly descend the stairs. The room became ghostly silent in an instant! Everyone's gaze fell on her. The men's jaws dropped to the floor as they cleared their throats and hastily gulped down their beverages. The women were flabbergasted and shocked as they gasped in amazement.

Magnolia Mae Moon was a sight such as had never been seen, not even by her husband. From her obsidian black, curly hair to her piercing blue eyes, to the touch of pink on her pearl white cheeks, to the pink lipstick on her luscious lips, to the fuchsia gown adorned with light pink roses and lace imported from France. Striking and imperial, she began greeting her guests: first the men, and then the women. As she walked away, she turned her bare shoulders to the red-blooded southern roosters, licking their lips with desire for her.

On the other hand, the women were appalled, filled with loathing and outright disgust at her gown, while hiding their reaction such as only southern women could.

After her grand entrance, and after scandalizing her female guests, she turned into a perfect hostess, chatting with everyone, exchanging pleasantries, discussing war strategies.

The band played all the classical favorites. The men and women broke into small groups. The men, of course, talked about the price of cotton and other staples that they grew. They compared strategies to control their slaves and how to get the most work out of them. Benjamin Hart said, in an intentionally louder voice, "I hear that Mrs. Moon, here, doesn't even refer to hers as slaves, but rather, *workers*! Honestly! Why on earth would she do that? It just shows that she knows nothing about running a plantation!"

Several of the men heartily agreed, and a few others begged to differ. "What difference does it make, as long as she gets an honest day's work out of them?"

"Easy," answered Mr. Hart. "If they get the idea that they're "workers," and not "slaves," they'll start demanding wages. Their own plot of land. And, who knows what else!" He continued, "But, perhaps that's what's happening here, eh? Perhaps she's having a difficult time with her SLAVES!

The entire room went quiet. Deathly quiet. Magnolia Mae didn't miss a beat. She pointed to the band leader, waved her hand, and he took her cue. He struck up a lively piece and said, "Time to dance, everyone! Gentlemen, take your lady onto the dance floor." And that was that.

As she waved good-bye to her very last guest, she exclaimed, "That will teach them! All of them!"

~~~~~~

One bright morning, the sun shone as it could only in the southern Georgia sky. The birds sang. A gentle breeze wafted through the pine trees. The majestic Magnolia dispensed a mixed fragrance of pine and jasmine into the air. Maggie Mae, still dressed in her night gown and shawl, sat in her rocker on the front porch as she did every morning. But this morning, something bothered her. She felt perturbed. She shivered, even though it wasn't at all chilly. She shifted in her rocker and tried to brush it off. But she couldn't.

Over yonder, she noticed a horseman dressed in light colored clothing. As he came closer and closer to the plantation pathway, she realized he was a Confederate soldier.

"Oh, my!" She rushed inside to get her robe. "Oh, my, oh, my, oh, my!" She ran up the stairs.

"Maggie? What's goin' on?" Flora asked.

"A Confederate soldier is a-comin'"

Flora quickly opened the front door and noticed how close the soldier was. "Hurry Maggie! He almost here!"

She stepped back and waited for her mistress to come back down to meet the soldier. The slaves were not allowed to interact with Confederate soldiers, who considered them ignorant and unworthy of being addressed.

As he reached the front porch, he dismounted, bowed, and tipped his hat. "Ma'am. Good mornin'." He pulled a white envelope from his horse's saddlebag.

"Good morning. What brings you here, kind sir?" She was still tying the ribbons on her robe—rather absentmindedly. She worked exceptionally hard to quell the trembling of her fingers. She was only partially successful. She knew full well why that Confederate soldier was on her doorstep. There could be only one reason.

"This is for you, ma'am. From the Army of the Confederate States of America." He handed her the envelope.

She took the envelope and looked at the seal. Her intuition was screaming at her while she worked to open it. Try as she might, the envelope simply refused to open. After what seemed to her like half a lifetime, she pulled the single sheet of paper from the envelope. As she began to read, she turned pale as a ghost. The paper fell from her hands. The soldier caught her as she started to collapse. "I'm so sorry, ma'am," was all he could say, choking back his own tears.

Chapter Seven

It seemed like forever for the mourning period to end. She had grown weary of wearing black dresses with black veils. The only thing she didn't grow tired of was the locket containing that lock of Roland's hair. Once in a while she pressed it very close to her heart or rubbed it between her fingers. At times she would open her husband's armoire and take in his aroma. She felt lost. Alone. Discarded. Sorrowful. Fearful. She mourned the passing of her husband, her lover, her soulmate. She was angry that her one true love would not even have a decent Christian funeral and burial. That hurt her the most. Oh, there was a funeral—of sorts, but with no body, it was simply a hollow sham. She also knew well that those landowners and so-called friends who showed up were simply being nice—all for show. Now came the storm. They were going to do anything and everything they could to force her out of her plantation and off her land.

"I'll be damned if I let them!" she shouted at the mirror one rainy morning.

But she had conjured up a plan during her mourning period and was about to put it in action. It was a known fact that when the head of a household died, the plantation needed to be passed down to a male heir. In her case, the male heir had just died, and her young son was not of age. So, she was now the successor of her parents' plantation. From immediately after the funeral, many a wealthy landowner would visit almost daily, asking to speak to Mrs. Moon. And every day, the answer was the same.

"She's in mournin' and she ain't comin' down." With their tail between their legs and resentment flowing in their veins, they would leave. Maggie Mae would peek out of her open bedroom window so she could eavesdrop.

"She's bound to come out sooner or later."

Or "She's just hidin' but this fine plantation will be mine. I just have ta wait."

"Over my dead body!" she would whisper back.

Or "Damn woman! She's avoidin' the unavoidable!"

These evil men were convinced by generations of tradition that a woman couldn't possibly take care of running a plantation or keeping the slaves at bay. That was a man's job.

"I am not going to let that happen," she said, quietly talking to herself in the mirror. "I will not sell what is rightfully mine." She finished pulling her hair up as she did every day. "Lord only knows where the slaves will go. They could be sold to other slaveowners or kept here, or they could even be separated." She plunged her soft puff pad inside the pink powder and lightly dabbed it on each cheek. She made sure not to overdo it as it was not proper for a well-to-do woman to put too much color on her face. "Oh, my! I just can't let that happen." She headed down to the parlor and sat in the wing chair. "Flora!" she shouted as she removed her veil. She wanted everyone to look her in the eyes when she made her proposal.

"Yes, Missy Maggie?"

"Can you kindly gather all the servants in here? I need to talk to all of y'all."

Flora bowed slightly. "Yes, missy Maggie." She quickly ran off.

While Maggie Mae waited patiently for the servants to assemble, she thought about what to say and how to say it. None of them had any real education, but she was determined to change that.

One by one, the male servants reached the front door. They removed their shoes or boots, removed their hats, and walked in. "Mornin,' " many of the men greeted their mistress as they bowed slightly. The room was slowly filling with servants, so much so, that she had some of the cleaner ones, the women mostly, sit on the sofas and chairs. They were extremely uncomfortable doing that because they had never been invited to do so by Mr. Moon, nor by the old folks.

"Are we lettin' in the children too, missy Maggie?"

"Yes, yes, everyone, please."

Flora collected all the servants' children and had them sit crossed legged on the rug, all in a row, while Maggie's two children each pulled out a dining room chair and made themselves comfortable.

Once everyone was settled in, she cleared her throat to speak. "Thank y'all for bein' here today." she took a deep breath. "As some of you may already know, with the passing of my husband, I am now in charge of this plantation." She looked up to see if there were any reactions. Nothing. "Some of you have been here since before I was born and some of you grew up with me and some of you young'ns grew up with my children." She looked at the children who gave her large, pearly white smiles. "Well, before you know it, some of my neighbors will be interested in buying this property from me because they believe that a woman does not have the ability or the smarts to run a plantation the way it should be run."

"Well, I beg to differ, missy Maggie. While your husband was a-fightin' in the war, why you took care of things 'round here just fine!"

"Yes, Charles, you are absolutely right. And this is the reason you're here today. I've been keeping an eye on things, and I don't believe the Confederacy is going to win this war. I thought so, from the very beginnin'. When the North wins, everyone is going to be freed. So, I have two choices to offer y'all at this time. The first is to let you go with your free-man papers so you can go up north and live your own free lives." A collective gasp permeated the room. "Or you can stay here with me and help me run this plantation the way it should be run."

Jonas, who was the eldest male Negro behind his father, piped up. "We ain't goin' nowhere, Missy Maggie, you is fam'ly to us. We loved yo' mama and daddy, and we love ya too." He knew quite well that he spoke for all of them.

"I understand, but before you make your decision, I want y'all to know how I feel about slavery. I don't think this is news to most of you, but I loathe it. I have never been able to suffer the indecency of it.

Treatin' y'all like you're nobody! Well, in my eyes and in the eyes of our Creator, you are his children just as much as I or any of my family are. I am in total agreement with President Lincoln when I say that I have never supported slavery and I never will."

To her pleasant surprise, everyone started clapping loudly. She smiled and waited patiently for everyone to stop clapping and pay attention once again.

"So, I have a proposal for y'all. If you agree to stay here and help me run this plantation, I will pay all the adults here a fair wage."

"A wage? But missy, but you ain't allowed to pay us negro folk." Charles exclaimed.

"I know that very well, Charles, but let me explain how I think this is gonna work."

"Well, all right, missy…"

"I asked around and found out that a fair wage is about five dollars per week for adults. Will that suit y'all?"

Each adult murmured yes or nodded. Charles was more vocal. "Yes, missy, daz a fine wage. I ain't never been paid ever in my life."

"Good to hear. Now, I'd like to pay the older children as well…I was thinkin' two dollars a week and once they are of age, they will receive the five. Is that all right for y'all?" she looked at the older children who mimicked the adults by simply nodding. "Very good. So, now comes the hard part. First, I need a commitment from each and every one of y'all that you'll stay here and work for me. I will prepare a contract and once you sign it, there's no turning back. Ya heah?"

"Well, I cain't sign my name. I ain't never learned how ta write." Chesney said.

"Never you mind, Chesney. All you need is to mark an X and that will make it legal."

"Datz easy. I can write an X."

"Now, the second part of my proposal, and I'm gonna warn ya, this is the most difficult part." She looked around the room. All their faces seemed to say, "hurry up now," without saying a word. "You will need to act like you're still my slaves. Can you do that?"

"I ain't understandin', missy, why would ya pay us a wage but keep us as yo' slaves?" This time Rose asked the question.

Maggie Mae stood up. "Because, if any of my neighbors or people of the town found out that I'm paying my slaves, they would lynch me along with each and every one of y'all." She looked at her children. "And my children would be sent to an orphanage, and they would divide every inch of this property among themselves. I'm sure that the Carsons or the Harts would love to possess my home, especially since theirs is much smaller and their families are much larger."

"We cain't have that missy!" Charles shook his head.

"No, Charles, we cannot." She paused. "You see, I love y'all and respect you as human beings. We are a family and I will not tolerate anyone treating you otherwise. Therefore, in order to keep face and to make this work, you must keep acting like you are my slaves. The only difference is that I will be paying you for your labor. You must also hide your earnings until the North wins this war and slavery is ended, once and for all."

"Missy Maggie, I know I is speakin' fa all of us when I saz dat we love ya, too, very much. You bin kin' ta us and even yo' parents and yo' husband, God rest dey souls, ain't never treated us bad. Dey was good people, dey was," Chesney said with tears streaming down her cheeks.

"That is exactly the reason that we need to keep this up. If anyone finds out that I am paying my slaves, it will be the end of Magnolia Blossom Plantation."

Everyone nodded.

"Thank you for understanding. Now, on to my third condition: I will educate your children along with mine. They will do their morning chores, and in the afternoon, I will teach them readin', writin' and 'rithmetic."

"But why? We ain't never needed no edacation." Charles asked.

"Because, when the south is free, and it will happen one day, mark my words, all children will need an education. You will need to be able to write, read, and perform basic math. This way the southern white man will not be able to swindle y'all. And he will, you can bet on it."

Yes, I s'pose you iz right."

"I know I am right, Flora. They try and do it to me all the time. And when your children begin to read you the stories they learn, you'll be very proud of them. I believe that to be true."

"Well, all right then." Flora replied.

"I have a final condition." She pulled a key out of her sleeve. "Pauly, would you mind goin' into your daddy's cabinet and getting' the guns?"

"Sure thing, Mama." He quickly took the key and ran to the parlor where the guns were kept under lock and key. He unlocked it and realized he could not possibly take them all. "I need some help."

Jupiter, Lewis, Harry, and Frankie quickly went to help him.

"Where do you want them, mama?" Pauly asked.

"Place them right there."

The boys placed the guns and rifles gently on the floor.

"These are for you men. I need you to protect this property. As the men of the family, it is your duty to protect us and everything we have."

"But we don't know how ta shoot. We ain't never shot natin'. Ever."

"Well, that's about to change." She got up and picked up a long gun. "I'd like each of you to go out back and learn how to shoot and that includes you older boys." She handed her gun to Charles. "Here, this one's yours. It was Daddy's favorite."

"I'm honored Missy Maggie Mae."

"That's quite all right. Now, the rest of y'all, pick one and learn how to use it. I want y'all to practice out back at the graveyard. Ain't nobody gonna heah ya there."

The men each picked up a gun, along with the older boys, just as Maggie Mae instructed. As they began to make their way to the back door, she stopped them.

"Before you go, I want y'all to sign these papers." She opened the small drawer of her writing desk and pulled out a small stack of papers. "These are your freedom papers."

"You got 'em ready?" Charles was surprised.

"Yes. I had plenty of time to prepare them while I was in mourning. There is one for each of you. I will read your freedom paper to you, and we both will sign them. This is your contract Charles. I will read it to you"

```
Know all men by these Presents that I,
Magnolia May Terry Moon, of the Town
of Valdosta in the State of Georgia,
for the sum of One Dollar ($1.00), do
hereby liberate and emancipate from
all manner of slavery. A certain Negro
man called Charles Willis and do
hereby allow him to possess his
freedom in full, clear from all claims
made or hereafter to be made by me, my
heirs, assigns, or any other person
under me claiming or demanding a right
to the person or services of the said
Charles Willis. Witness my hand & seal
this eighth day of October in the year
of Our Lord Eighteen Hundred and
Sixty-two.

Magnolia Mae Terry - Moon (Seal)
```

Magnolia Mae took the pen from the desk and dipped it into the small ink bottle. She signed the paper and then handed him the pen.

"Well…" he took the pen, "Are you sure 'bout this?"

"Yes, Charles, I'm very sure." She stood up. "You're my family and you're the only family I have left." She turned to the rest of the group. "Please allow me to treat you as my family. I have no one, only y'all." She sat back down and waited for Charles to sign the sheet.

He scribbled something vaguely resembling a signature and then gave the pen back to Maggie Mae. "Is that all right?"

"Perfect." She turned the page over and pointed to a number. "There, that's your wage. It says five dollars. See that is a number five and those are two zeros, meaning no cents. And these are real dollars." She opened up another smaller drawer and pulled out five single dollar bills.

Charles had never seen money before. He had seen it being exchanged between his master and his business partners when he accompanied him to Valdosta, but he had never actually touched it. He recognized the number one, but he didn't recognize anything else. It was made of fine paper, just like the one he just signed. It had a picture of a steamship, a lady holding a banner over her head, another lady's face, some letters, and other designs. He examined it closely and then turned it over to look at the other side. "Missy Maggie Mae, I trust ya, believe me, I do an' I ain't goin' anywhere. I'm gonna stay and earn my wage. C'mon ya'll, come fawad an' sign these heah papers."

That is exactly what the group needed. Their leader was the only person who could convince them that they were doing the right thing by signing up to stay with Maggie Mae. They had trusted her parents all their lives so why not trust her now? One by one, all the adults, came forward and wrote an X on the line. As they did that, Maggie Mae, distributed the bills. Each signee looked over the Confederate bills and, same as Charles, turned them over and over again, fascinated by the currency.

Maggie Mae smiled as her heart filled with joy and her eyes with tears. She didn't see the color of their skin. She saw only members of one family. Her family.

Chapter Eight

As Lieutenant Wesley Joshua Jenkins rode into Georgia with his 55th Brigade of New York, his grandfather's stories slid into his memory.

Abeo Obinna was a prince in Nigeria who was kidnapped by slave-traders and brought to Georgia at the very young age of ten. Although he was re-named Abe Jenkins by his master, as was customary in those days, he refused to be treated as a slave. His pride and stubbornness ended up getting him flogged and beaten constantly. One evening, when he was fifteen, he collected some food and clothes and ran away with his faithful dog. Although he was hunted down all the way to Maryland, he found refuge with a former slave community that lived together and free, in the outskirts of Baltimore. He grew strong, proud, and most importantly—free. He married Kanika, who was the daughter of a former slave and had taken a liking to Abe. She was 15 and he was 16. They settled in New York where they became involved with the Underground

Railroad, helping many slaves flee the southern states and find freedom in the Northern states and Canada. They would have 6 children. His son Joshua was the father of Wesley Joshua Jenkins.

Wesley's brigade was ordered to settle in Valdosta as to set them up strategically to fight off the Confederates and push them into Florida where there were other Union troops waiting eagerly to fight the cause and win the Civil War.

As they rode through the state, Wesley took notes: about the terrain, the many plantation homes he encountered, and the multiple slave families that secretly gave them refuge. He needed their help because he and his brigade were all free black men, hence placing themselves in a high risk of danger for two reasons: they were Union soldiers and they were Negroes.

Maggie Mae was sitting on the back porch listening to her son read, when she heard Charles approach.

"Miss Maggie Mae?"

"Yes, Charles. What's goin' on?"

"There's sum ho'ses comin' up the way headin' to the house."

She shot up and ordered: "You two! To your rooms, right now! And don't come out until I tell ya' to, ya hear?"

"Yes, mama." They said at the same time as they collected their things and hurried up the back stairs to their rooms.

"And hide in your wardrobes, like we practiced!" she barked. Then she turned to Ned. "Now, we talked about this right? I need you to get all the men with the guns and go to the front porch!" She headed to the gun cabinet and pulled out the two smaller guns that her father had given to her when she was a child. After she'd had the talk with her slaves, she asked Charles to teach her how to shoot—and became quite good at it.

Charles called onto the fields. "Ya'll need ta come to da house ra't now!"

The men dropped their tools and quickly gathered in front of Charles.

"There's trouble a-comin' our way and y'all need ta go git your guns and git on the front porch alongside of Miss Maggie Mae! Now git!"

They all went running off and into their respective cabins. Only a few seconds went by and all the men scurried out to be with their matriarch on the front porch.

All of them had been trained to shoot by Charles, and all of them had become expert shooters.

"Good. Y'all are here." She collected her thoughts as she noticed there was only one carriage heading down the plantation pathway. "Let's do this: young'ns, go hide behind those bushes, and you go to that side of the house. Charles, Cato, Ned, and Willy, y'all go wait inside and stay behind the front door until you hear me say…um…slaves come. Y'all understand?"

"Yes'm," replied Ned as all the men took their positions.

The carriage, led by two horses, pulled up and stopped right in front of Maggie Mae. The driver got down and opened the carriage door, letting Benjamin Hart and his son James step out.

Maggie Mae wanted to shoot both men right then and there, but she stayed seated on her rocking chair, covering her pistol with her fan, while her second smaller pistol was discretely inserted in her leg holster that Rose had made specially for her.

"Good Morning Mrs. Moon." Benjamin slightly bowed and removed his hat. James did the same. "Lovely October mornin' isn't it?"

"Yes, quite warm for this time a year. What brings you here on this fine day?" She remained seated with her hand gently touching the hidden pistol.

James thought she was still a vision, even if she was still wearing her black mourning clothes. Her luscious red lips popped out under her veil, along with her black curls. Although he still was furious with her for refusing to marry him for that jackass Roland, he figured she could still be a perfect wife for him after he had her bastards sent away to some orphanage. He did not want to share his potential inheritance with bastard children; he wanted only ***his*** children to have everything he owned.

"Mrs. Moon, we've come here today with a proposal."

She had a bad feeling about this and tried to hide her concern. "What type of proposal?"

Benjamin fanned himself with his hat. "Could we step inside? It's awfully hot out here?"

She loved seeing him sweat and slither, just like the snake in the grass he was. "Well, I'm afraid that's not possible, Mr. Hart. As you well know, the mourning period is not over yet, and it would not be proper for a widow to entertain two men inside the house. Wouldn't you agree?"

"Well, I suppose you're right." He kept on fanning himself.

"Well, all right then, may I hear your proposal?" she really didn't want to hear anything he had to say, but her daddy had taught her to be polite.

"Many years ago, you decided to marry your deceased husband instead of accepting James' proposal."

"I did." She looked at James. He was still quite handsome with his muscular build, chestnut eyes, and dark brown hair. But he still had that evil look in his eyes that had deterred her from accepting his proposal in the first place.

"Well, now that you are available again, I would like to request your hand in marriage again, if I may?" James asked.

Her eyes widened as her lips tightened. A shiver went down her spine. *Of course, he wants to marry me now that I have more to offer. My plantation, my slaves, and all my possessions will be his. Oh, I can see the look of greed in his eyes. Over my dead body!* She thought carefully about her answer. "Well, bless yo' heart and I must say I am very flattered by your proposal…" she stood up grasping her pistol with her right hand and covering it with her fan. "but the mourning period is not over yet. How could I possibly remarry?"

"I'll take a promise for now. Then, once the mourning is done, we can marry. Do you agree?"

No! I will never marry you!

"Mr. Hart, I do appreciate the proposal, I do but I'm afraid I can't marry you."

You whore!

"Oh? But why?" James asked trying to hide his fury.

"Mr. Hart, I don't want to offend you, but the answer is quite simple."

"Please, Mrs. Moon, I do not offend easily." He wasn't offended; he was fuming.

"Mr. Hart, I don't love you. I am terribly sorry, but if I ever do remarry, and frankly, I don't see it happening, it must be for love."

"Mrs. Moon, I understand. But if I may ask, is there someone else?"

"Why, no, of course not! I am still very much in love with my Roland and I simply do not see myself loving someone else. I hope you understand."

No. He didn't understand.

"Mrs. Moon, if I may intercede." Benjamin asked.

"Yes, Mr. Hart."

"In my opinion, you need to remarry. You need a man in your household. You need a man who will take over your plantation, your slaves, your crops and all your affairs. It is not proper for a woman to take all this upon herself. It would be too much for you to handle."

"Is that so?" She was about ready to put a bullet in his head, but she kept calm.

"Of course. Running a plantation is no job for a woman." His beady little eyes jeered at her.

"I see. Well, Mr. Hart, I'd like to ask you a question now. If I may."

Benjamin was beginning to lose his temper trying to convince this widow to marry his son. "Please."

"I'd like you to look around and tell me what you see."

He didn't want to waste any more time with her games, but he humored her. He looked around the front yard, the flower garden, the pathway and noticed it looked as it should. No weeds, flowers blooming, trees trimmed, pathway gravel neat and tidy. "Looks in order."

"And who do you think managed to keep the plantation in order?"

"I s'pose it was you." He frowned, as he knew where she was headed.

"Exactly. My husband has been gone for over six months now and I do believe *my* plantation is very well kept. Don't you agree, Mr. Hart?"

"I s'pose."

"And you do see me goin' to market quite often, don't ya? I bring my crops, I bargain as my daddy taught me, I buy supplies. I want of nothin'. Isn't that right Mr. Hart?"

"Yes, I have seen you quite often goin' 'bout your business."

"Well, then, what makes you think that I need a man here?" she asked politely trying to keep her temper in check.

"You don't at this moment, but you will. Sooner or later you won't be able to handle your business any longer and you will need to remarry. I only hope that James here will be your choice."

"Well, I do thank you for your consideration. But for right now, I think I am handlin' things quite well. Therefore, if you don't mind, I best be getting' back to schoolin' my children. Good day, Mr. Hart. James."

Benjamin decided to show her authority. "Mrs. Moon, I can have you removed from this land by the authorities, and believe me I will if you continue in your recalcitrant ways."

"Are you threatenin' me, Mr. Hart?"

Benjamin was about to open his mouth, but James took a step forward and waved him off. "Mrs.

Moon, please, do not be upset. My father wants only what's best for me, is all." He stepped a bit closer as Maggie Mae took a step back. "Listen, I understand that you're still mourning and that's the way it should be. But please take my proposal into consideration, as I would be honored to be your husband and help you run your plantation."

Even though his words seemed sincere, his demeaner was not. The evil in his eyes became more prominent as Maggie Mae felt another shiver go down her spine. She faked a smile and said, "Mr. Hart, I sincerely appreciate your concern and believe me, your proposal is quite flattering, but I ask you for some time to ponder on it. May I?"

"All the time you need, Mrs. Moon." He turned to his father. "Father and I will return in a few months to check up on ya, if that's all right with you."

"Yes, that would be fine." She took another step back.

The Harts bowed and placed their hats on their heads. As the driver opened the carriage door, James said; "Have a pleasant day, Mrs. Moon." They entered, and the driver closed the door.

"Do you want to tell me what that was all about?"

"Now, father, you of all people should know that you catch more flies with honey than with vinegar."

Benjamin grumbled something under his breath as he sat back.

"I have ta sweeten her up. I have ta court her. She's a very tough woman and she needs tamin' just like Sir William Shakespeare's Shrew."

"I s'pose."

"Let me take care of this situation. I'll make ya proud Father, I promise. I'll have her eatin' out of the palm of my hand in no time. And when we're finally married…and we will be…I assure ya…I'll send those bastards packin' and beat her until she has no choice but to obey me." Then he sat back, closed his eyes, and imagined his life with the most beautiful woman of Valdosta by his side.

Maggie Mae didn't move a muscle until the carriage was out of sight. She exhaled. "All right, y'all can come out now."

The front door opened, and the elder workers came out while the younger men came out of their hiding places.

"You dun handled yo'self well, Missy Maggie."

"Yes, Charles, I believe I did, but they'll be back. And it will get harder and harder to fend them off."

"Yes'm, Miss Maggie, I s'pose so."

Maggie Mae shielded her eyes from the midday sun with her hand. "Looks like it's lunchtime. Chesney, I hope you made sum of your delicious collard greens, cuz I'm famished."

Chapter Nine

Lieutenant Jenkins was scrutinizing the area in search of a place in a strategic area. Even though it was very early in the year 1863, the temperature was not anything like what the cold Northern winters had to offer. On the contrary, ever since he entered Georgia back in October, he was rather enjoying the climate that his grandfather's home state was offering. His men were down by the creek, resting and preparing food, while he rode on for a bit. He stumbled upon a holy field. He dismounted his horse and got down on one knee to read the headstone.

Here lies George Paul Terry. Born April 10, 1799 – Died December 1, 1860.

Right next to that one was what seemed to be his wife's headstone.

Here lies Anita Sarah Terry. Born July 22, 1801 – Died November 19, 1860.

"They died eleven days apart. I wonder what happened." He got up, removed his hat, and used his sleeve to rub the sweat off his brow.

"Who are you?"

He turned to find a young girl peering at him with ocean blue eyes, reddish curly hair, sneering, with her hands on her hips.

"Lieutenant Wesley Joshua Jenkins at your service, Miss." He removed his hat and bowed, slightly.

"Well, you shouldn't be here. You need to leave, now!" she demanded.

Amused by her attitude, he tried to be as gentle as possible. "I may leave, but I may stay too. I haven't decided just yet."

"Don't move! I'm gonna git Charles." And she ran off yelling "Charles! Charles!"

Perhaps he's her father. No, she wouldn't call him Charles.

Nary a few minutes passed, and the little girl was storming in his direction, but this time, she had a black man with white hair holding her hand.

"See, Charles, I told ya. There he is." She pulled him, but he stopped her.

"Miss Lizzy, please go on back to da house, now, come on." He released her and gently pushed her toward the main house.

"Oh, but why?"

"Never you mind. Go to Mammy and stay dere. Ya heah?"

"Yes, sir." She bowed her head as she walked away disappointed.

"You a Yankee?" noticing the uniform.

"Yes, sir, Lieutenant Wesley Joshua Jenkins at your service." Once again bowing and removing his hat.

"A Negro soldier? I ain't never seen no Negro soldier. Whatcha doin' 'round here, boy?"

"I believe your name is Charles. Pleased to meet you, sir." He held his hand out.

"Sir? I ain't no sir. Nobody ever dun call me dat."

"Well, you are my senior and I was taught to call all men senior to me sir."

"Whatcha doin' in dese here parts anyhow?"

"Well, Charles, if I may call you that." He paused, waiting for some kind of response. Charles remained motionless. "I'm here to win this war, sir."

"Win dis war? Ain't no Negro gonna win dis war."

"Whose side are you on, sir? You're a slave and we are fighting to rid the south of slavery. Don't you want your freedom sir? Do you want to be a slave for that old white man living in that mansion for the rest of your life?" pointing at the house.

Charles laughed, mildly at first. But that morphed into a deep laugh—so hard that tears formed in his eyes.

"What's so funny?"

Charles just kept on laughing. He couldn't stop.

"Come on, old man, why are you laughing?" Lieutenant Jenkins was obviously irritated by now.

"That old white man is me." Maggie Mae had snuck up behind the Lieutenant.

When Wesley turned, he froze. He was facing the most beautiful and captivating blue-eyed, curly-haired creature he had ever met in his entire life, aiming a Belgium Pinfire revolver with an ivory grip at his face. His mouth was open wide, but his tongue was frozen.

"Cat got your tongue, Lieutenant?" she asked sensually, while keeping the pistol securely in both her hands.

Indeed, it felt like it. Wesley threw his hands up in the air, swallowed, and cleared his throat. "No, ma'am."

"Seems like it ta me." Charles was grinning like a Cheshire Cat.

"I'm sorry, ma'am, you caught me off guard." He did not move.

"You may put your hands down, but if you even go near that pistol, I'll put a bullet between your eyes."

"Yes, ma'am." He brought his hands down to his side. He was pretty sure she would have kept her promise.

"Now, tell me, Lieutenant. What're you doin' here?"

"Well, ma'am, my brigade and I are searching for a strategic area to set up camp and I stumbled across this here holy field."

"I see." She looked down at her parents' graves. "And where are your men, now?" the pistol was still pointing at his face.

"They're down by the creek, ma'am. They're tired and I ordered them to rest a bit."

Maggie Mae had never seen a Union soldier, not to mention a black one, but there was something very different about this man. His eyes were full of kindness and his demeanor was proud, but gentle. He had an almost royal air about him. He was quite different from the black men she had grown up with—including Charles, who was like a second father to her. He was tall and not too slim. His skin was not as dark as the blacks she knew; his was lighter. Perhaps it was due to the cold, hard winters of the North that made even the darkest skinned white folk turn pale white.

"I see. Well, what do you want?"

"As I was telling Charles here, I am here to win this war and bring freedom to the black people in the south, just as our President ordered." How he wished she would lower that pistol.

She admired this soldier. His cause was the right one, and the one she had always agreed with. Regardless, she needed to show caution, especially since she and her two children were the only white people on the plantation.

"Well, all right. I don't mind you and your men restin' for a while on my land, but you need to leave as soon as you can, ya heah?"

"Yes, ma'am, I understand but my men are tired. May I ask if we can stay for a couple of days?"

"To be honest, I don't mind you stayin' at all, but I hope you realize that you are in Confederate country and if they find y'all, you'll be dead faster than green grass through a goose."

Wesley cracked a smile at her. She was a true southern belle.

"What's so funny?" she stretched the pistol closer to his face.

"I am sorry ma'am; I didn't mean no disrespect, but I've never heard that before. I'm from New York, and we don't talk like that."

"Well, I suppose it can be funny. New York, ya say? Well, I won't hold that against you." She smiled warmly. "Now, please leave. I don't want any bloodshed on my property." Finally, she put her pistol down. "Good day, Lieutenant." She turned on her heels and headed towards the house.

"Best do what she tell ya," Charles called out over his shoulder as he too, headed for the house.

~~~~~~

Charles awoke to the sound of rapping on the door.

"Who dat?" Harriet asked, still groggy.

"I dunno but I best go check. Cud be Missy Maggie…" he dressed quickly, turned up the flame on the lantern, picked up his rifle, and made his way to the door. He waited a few seconds. He wanted to make sure he wasn't hearing things. Another knock showed that he wasn't. He opened the door. "Whatcha doin' here boy?"

Wesley gently pushed the old man aside and entered the cabin. "We need to talk, sir."

Charles closed the door and pointed his rifle at him. "Ain't nuttin' to talk 'bout."

But Wesley was not looking to leave; he looked for a place to sit. "What I have to tell you is very important."

"Charles? Waz goin' on? Whoz dis man?" then the light shone on Wesley, and clearly showed his uniform. "A Yankee? A Negro Yankee?" She rubbed her eyes, not believing what they were telling her. Then she put her hands on her hips. "Charles, waz goin' on here? Whoz dis Negro Yankee?"

"Harriet, you best go back ta bed. I'll handle dis."

"No, she can stay. What I have to say is for every one of you black folk to hear." He got up and pulled another chair out for Harriet. "Please, ma'am, have a seat."

Grumbling she took her seat but pulled it farther away from Wesley. Even if he was black, he was still a Yankee.

"Well, go on. State your biznis, Negro." Charles did not sit. He stayed standing, rifle in hand and at the ready.

"The reason why I was on this property earlier today is because I was looking for a strategic spot to plant my brigade so we can move forward and send the Confederates down into Florida, gaining some valuable ground."

"I don git war tauk boy."

"All right, well, basically we are going to push the rebels into Florida and this place is perfect for us to make our base camp."

"So? Waz it got da do wid us?"

"In order to keep our base here, we need to take over your barracks and make them our own."

"Huh? And where we goin'?"

"Well that's the important news, we are going to free you. All of you. From bondage."

"Free? Us?" Harriet asked.

"Yes, the Union will declare you free people and you can leave this plantation. Go up north where all of us are free."

"Ya don't look free to me. That uniform binds ya ta da Yankees. Y'ain't free son, you just have a different massa, is all."

"I assure you, sir, that I chose to become a Union soldier. I was not drafted. I chose to fight for this cause, and I chose to stand up for what is right. President Lincoln wants the south to free slaves and the Confederates don't. Can't you see?"

"Well, ya cain't free us cuz we already free."

"What are you saying, old man?"

"I'm sayin' we is free and we earnin' a wage, too."

Wesley was flabbergasted at what he just heard! *How could that be? Who freed these people? What conditions were contrived?* Surely, that white woman has them buffaloed! "A wage? You mean like pay? Who's paying you? I'm not understanding."

"Yessir. Miss Maggie is paying us a wage." Charles made the statement with pride.

"You mean to tell me that the woman pointing a gun at me this morning is paying you a wage?"

"Yes, exactly."

"She's a widow, ya know," Harriet clarified.

Wesley recalled the tombstones of what seemed like her parents, but he didn't see a third fresh grave. "Is her husband buried up there?"

"Na. They nev'r sent him home. They buried him in a commun grave. All she got was his belongins, is all."

A wave of sympathy and pity came over Wesley. He was beginning to see clearly. "So, you mean to tell me she's a widow who is running this plantation all on her own?"

"No. With our help. We ain't slaves no mo', we's workers an' we git paid a wage."

"Well, let me ask you this: has she paid you already?"

"Yessir." Harriet went to the bedroom, shuffled around and came back pulling a five-dollar bill from her bosom. "See. Dis is a fi' dolla bill an' it's ours." She waved it in front of his face.

"Well, how about that." He took a detailed, close-up look at it. "It's authentic, from what I can see."

"Sho' is."

"Won't do you any good though. It's not Union currency, its valid only in the south."

"Well, dat's fine cuz we ain't goin' up north. Wez stayin' raht cheer with Miss Maggie Mae an' we gonna work on dis here land."

"But you'll have real freedom up north, and you'll make real money."

"Now, you best save y'ur breath boy. We'z ain't goin' nowhere, we'z stayin' raht cheer, an' dat's final."

Harriet got up and walked up to Wesley. "Now, you look like a good boy. Is yo' a good boy? Oh, I'm sure your mama is mighty proud a' ya."

"I suppose she is." He also stood up as a courtesy.

"Well, good. Now, I'm gonna give ya sum advice, as y'ur mama wud. Go on, sit." She commanded gently.

Wesley sat slowly wondering what this old woman had to say. He nodded.

"Ya see, Miss Maggie Mae is a widow with two young'ns, an' just befo' she became widow, she lost both her mama and papa, too. God rest their souls. They was gud folk, they was. They dun always treated us with respect. We was der fam'ly, we was no slaves, we was fam'ly." She went to the stove, threw in a log, and put a kettle on. "My girl, Flora, she's Miss Maggie's best friend and she's her personal maid, too. They love each udder, just like real siblins."

"She right. All our chirr'n are like brothers and sisters to Miss Maggie and she's like 'ar own daughter. Ya git me son?" Charles chimed in.

"Yes, I'm starting to see now, but I still…"

"Yessir, you gots mo' questions, and rightfully so."

Wesley nodded at Charles while Harriet poured some tea for all three.

"Ya see, we dun made a pac' with Missy Maggie."

"What kind of pact?" Wesley sipped his tea quietly.

"We stayin' and pretendin' to be her slaves while she payin' us a wage."

"A wage? Why would she do that?"

"Fo' protection. She a white, widow raisin' her youngins and runnin' dis 'ere plantation. We gots ta protect 'er; fo her daddy an' mama but 'specially fa her protection. We just caint abandon 'er, we caint. Ya see now, son?"

Wesley sipped his tea while he pondered what the old man had said. It made sense now. The black folk here were not true slaves. They were a family, and he couldn't tear apart a family. He shook his head. He'd never heard of such a thing before! Suddenly, he felt a profound respect and admiration for the beautiful Maggie Mae Moon. He got up. "Well, I'd best be going." He headed for the door. "I have to think about this, and I will return to pay a visit to Mrs. Moon." He opened the door, tipped his hat, and vanished into the night.

~~~~~~

"Well, all right, let's do some arithmetic." Maggie Mae passed around some papers to the children that were sitting around the dining room table. "No peeking on other young'ns, ya heah? Do the exercise by yourselves."

There was a loud knock on the front door.

"Charles, would you mind seein' who it is?"

"Yes'm, Miss Maggie Mae." He headed for the hallway, opened the door and saw Wesley standing there with his hat in his hand.

"Good morning, Mr. Willis, how are you today?" he smiled.

"I'm all right." Charles wasn't smiling. He thought he'd never see the Union soldier ever again, but he was wrong.

"I'd like to have a word with Mrs. Moon, if I'm not disturbing."

"I'm gonna see if she's available. You wait here boy."

Wesley nodded as Charles shuffled towards the back of the house. Wesley couldn't help but notice the aroma of something cooking in the kitchen. His stomach growled. He took a few steps forward and noticed the luxury of the rugs, furnishings, the pictures and all decorations typical of rich Victorian homes. The house was immaculate and looked like nobody lived in it.

"Lieutenant Jenkins. To what do I owe the courtesy of your visit?" Maggie Mae appeared from the back of the house looking as stunning and as sensual as ever. His hunger was replaced with want…for her.

"Um…ah…Mrs. Moon, it is a pleasure to see you again." He bowed.

Although she too enjoyed seeing him again and she too had to hide her attraction to this noble looking black man. She curtsied. "Would you like to come and sit down?" she pointed to her parlor.

"Yes, that would be fine. Thank you." Holding his hat between his fingers, he followed her into the parlor and sat in one of the wing chairs.

"You must be parched. May I get you some sweet tea?"

Those lips, those eyes…he had to stop looking at her. "Yes, thank you, ma'am."

"Fanny, could you please bring some sweet tea to the Lieutenant?"

"Yes'm." Fanny was waiting just outside the parlor. She knew her role well since she was the oldest slave woman.

"So, what brings you here, Lieutenant?"

"Well, if you remember we met near your parent's grave." He hesitated. He didn't want to set her off. He needed to be very diplomatic about what he was going to propose to her.

"Yes, I remember."

"Well, the reason I was there is because I was searching for a strategic place to set up my battalion and battle the Confederates by pushing them as far out of Georgia as we possibly can." He examined her carefully to see her reaction.

"I see." She simply replied as Fanny appeared with a tray carrying a pitcher of sweet tea and two glasses.

"Just lay them there, thank you Fanny." She picked up the pitcher and poured the tea in both glasses. She picked one up and handed it to Wesley. As they touched, a spark was felt.

He was lost for words. That spark was felt in his deep insides. He gulped half of his tea down.

Maggie Mae sipped it slowly. "Please continue Lieutenant."

"Huh? Oh, yes, of course." He placed his glass on the tray. "I have determined that this plantation is perfect for our plans." He looked at the designs on the Persian rug.

"Do you mean to tell me that y'all are gonna take over my plantation?" she was irritated. *The gall of this Yankee!*

"Well, yes and no."

"Now, whatev'r does that mean?" she was confused.

"Yes, my intention is to take over your plantation BUT, I won't do anything without your permission." This time he looked into her oceanic colored eyes.

"Well, then, no need to continue this conversation. My answer is no." she got up.

Wesley also rose. "Please, Mrs. Moon, hear me out. Please?"

She sat back down. "Well, all right then. I s'pose I owe you that much."

"I know about the pact you made with your slaves."

She raised her eyebrows. "You do? And how did you find out?"

"Well, you see, a few days ago I paid a visit to Charles and Harriet and they explained your situation."

"Oh?" she didn't know what else to say. She was surprised to say the least.

"I was sincerely moved by the loyalty and dedication they have for you. They explained that you and your slaves are family."

"Yes, Lieutenant, that is correct. My parents did things much differently than our neighbors." She took another sip of tea. "Ya see, while the other plantation owners beat, flogged and worked their slaves to death, my daddy treated his with respect and dignity. In fact, our plantation flourished so much that our crops were most abundant and of the best quality in Valdosta. They could never figure out how my daddy did it and I'll tell you another thing; best they never found out or my daddy would have been lynched right alongside of his slaves." She shuddered at that thought.

"And they never suspected a thing?"

"No, sir. My parents threw the most lavish parties with the best food and wine in the whole state of Georgia, I assure you. When those slaveowners were around, our slaves acted just like any of theirs but once they were outta sight, we became a family again."

"That is most impressive. You certainly are not what I had expected."

"Well, thank you, Lieutenant."

"Now, I have an offer to make you and I truly hope you'll accept."

His eyes were kind. She could see there was no malice in this man's soul. "I'm listenin'."

"If you allow my battalion and myself to build a base, we, in turn, will provide protection, will help your slaves work your land and we will push the rebels down into Florida."

Maggie Mae was flabbergasted at his offer but she thought about it. She certainly could use the manpower since she was probably the only woman who ran a plantation in Valdosta. Not to mention, she loathed slavery and wanted it abolished. She did have questions. "Lieutenant, have you considered that fact that my neighbors will report you to the authorities if they discover your base? You do understand that they will take possession of my land and have me and my children banned from this state."

"Yes, Mrs. Moon, I have considered the risks. Firstly, we will build barracks down towards the creek and this will allow us to not be seen by the Rebels or your neighbors for that matter."

"What about your uniforms? You can tell from very far away that you're Yankees. Why, the Confederates will attack you in the middle of the night and Lord know what they'll do to me and my children. I cannot take this risk." She stood up again.

Wesley had to think quickly. He was losing her. "Wait, please, I have an idea."

"What idea?" she didn't sit; she just waited for him to speak.

"What if we didn't wear our uniforms, rather, dress like your slaves. You see, all my men are black and we would fit right in. What do you say?"

She sat down. "Oh, that could work."

"Yes, yes, we would only wear them when we are in battle and when we are on the premises, we will store them away. We can build boxes inside the walls of the barracks made of cedar to store and hide our uniforms while we pretend to be your slaves." He spoke quickly as the ideas rolled off his tongue.

She was quiet for several seconds. She was imagining how this could work. "How many men do you have Lieutenant?"

"Fifty-seven at the moment."

Maggie Mae let it sink in then she burst out laughing, at first quite low then she got louder.

"What is so funny, Mrs. Moon?"

"ha ha…I'm sorry, Lieutenant...ha ha..." she recomposed herself. "Can you imagine having fifty-five slaves all of a sudden show up on my plantation? And all men at that." She continued to laugh. "Well, the other slaveowners would become insanely jealous and wonder how I managed to buy fifty-seven male slaves. Why their heads would explode!"

Wesley did find that funny and cracked a smile. He found her laugh to be very sensual and alluring. "All right, so, do we have a deal then?"

"Lieutenant Jenkins, you have yourself a deal." She got up and stretched her hand to him.

He removed his white glove and instead of shaking it, he kissed it. "Wonderful. We will begin building right away." He headed for the door.

"Lieutenant Jenkins, would you like to stay for supper? This way we can make more plans."

Without hesitation. "Mrs. Moon, I would be delighted."

Chesney and Harriet looked at each other in disarray. They knew it in their bones that this agreement would only lead to trouble.

Chapter Ten

After barely a few days, the barracks were beginning to rise. A total of three were laid out by the creek. Oddly enough, the brigade had enough building supplies with them. Maggie Mae found out that it was the intent of the Union General to have this brigade build a settlement once they found a strategic place.

When the brigade was not working on the barracks, they mingled with the plantation slaves. The young black girls were courted by the younger black Union soldiers, while the younger black boys were being indoctrinated with Union propaganda slowly turning the Confederacy into a new enemy. The very young black children, along with Maggie Mae's two children, were kept inside the mansion and home-schooled by Maggie Mae herself, just as she promised at the signing.

Wesley and his subordinate officers were laying out attack plans to strategically push the Rebels down into Florida, where another Union brigade was waiting to take them over. It was known that the Confederates were low on money, supplies, and able-bodied men. They had been recruiting black men, along with very young southern men; some not even sixteen yet. Since younger men and black men were very inexperienced in shooting or following orders, they were losing more and more battles. President Lincoln knew well his army was winning, but at the same time, he was saddened by the great loss of young men on both sides.

Along with building supplies, Lieutenant Jenkins had a sufficient supply of food to last him for over three months, and the kitchen women were grateful. Nonetheless, the plantation's vegetable garden's size was doubled within about two months of the brigade being there.

Flora, Lana, Chesney, Fanny, and Lily were kept busy by the increase of cooking and cleaning that needed to be done, especially with the increase in hungry young men buzzing around.

Rose, Molly, and Harriet kept busy with laundry and mending the Union uniforms.

During the day, the troops were working the land while Charles and the other "workers" did everything else that needed doing around the plantation, like milking the cows, cleaning the stables, picking and washing vegetables, and keeping the property in pristine condition.

Wesley met with Maggie Mae many times during those three months—so much, that it had become a ritual. They would sit in the parlor, have tea, and chat about all sorts of things. Wesley would recount the stories his grandfather told him as a child, while Maggie Mae listened in awe. On the other hand, Maggie Mae gave him the history of the Magnolia Blossom Plantation. Those meetings went from being just a few minutes long to being hours long—all the while, developing a dangerously close relationship as well. Everyone was noticing, especially Harriet, and she was not pleased.

~~~~~~

On a brisk Monday morning in early March, Maggie Mae, Charles, and Wesley embarked to go to Valdosta with a heaping crop of cotton that had been just sorted in the gin and loaded on the wagon.

"Mrs. Moon, are you sure about this?"

"Yes, Lieutenant, positive." She held her head high while she held on to Wesley's arm, as Charles drove the wagon on the dusty road. She had asked both Wesley and Charles to accompany her to town, since she wanted to officially be seen with a new slave in the hopes that any slaveowner desiring to kick her out of her property would be disillusioned and leave her be. She still wore black with matching gloves and hat, but she had removed her veil.

"What if someone asks me where I come from?"

"Simple. The land of your granddaddy. Why, you've told me time and time again that you even remember the language that your granddaddy spoke. Well, now's the time to speak it."

"Yes, I can try."

"Ain't nobody gon' talk to ya, son. Them slaveowners never say nothin' to us Negro folk. Jus' keep yer head low and don't look anyone in da eye. Ya got dat?"

Wesley nodded.

"Ya learn quick. Da's good, son."

Wesley had never been to Valdosta and marveled at how unsophisticated it was. He also searched for strategic vantage points to take it over. He noticed a hotel named "Valdosta Grand Hotel", a couple of saloons, the sheriff's office with the jail inside, a farmer's market, a general store, and other buildings.

Charles stopped in front of the cotton market. He climbed off the wagon and then helped Maggie down.

"Now, you two Negros stay here while I go inside." She winked at them as she said it. She turned on her heels, lifted her skirt slightly, so to not show anything above the ankle, and headed for the market courtyard.

Mr. Steward was about to enter the courtyard as well but when he saw Maggie Mae, he stopped, tipped his hat, and held the gate open for her. "Mrs. Moon."

"Well, good mornin' Mr. Steward. And how are you this fine day?" she put on her sweetest, southern belle voice.

"I'm doin' fine." He placed his hat back on his head and looked over to her slaves. "Is that a new Negro I see?"

"Why, yes, that is. Bought him just a few weeks ago."

Mr. Steward peered at her unconvinced. "You didn't buy him here, we ain't had no auction in a long time."

Caught a bit off guard. "Un…in Atlanta…we went to Atlanta. That's about the only place you can buy one these days with this awful war goin' on."

As she headed for the main desk, Mr. Steward shook his head behind her back. *That woman is a liar.*

"Good morning, Mr. Grady, Mr. Barnes, Mr. Dunbar, Mr. Davidson and Mr. Stone. How are y'all this fine mornin'?"

All five men removed their hats and bowed to greet her while mumbling their greetings. She walked into the marketplace as if she owned the place, walking straight up to the head auctioneer.

"Good mornin' Mr. Cooke. How are you this fine day?" she was perky. She knew well that Mr. Cooke had a soft spot for her because of her captivating beauty, but also because he had just lost his wife to cholera and was beginning to search for her replacement.

"Mrs. Moon…" he kissed her hand covered with her black glove. "What brings you here on this lovely morning?"

"Well, Mr. Cooke, if you can kin'ly follow me, I'd be happy to show ya." She gave him an alluring smile and headed for her wagon.

He didn't need to be told twice. He followed her just like a puppy dog behind his new master.

"Here. This is why I'm here." she pointed at her abundant crop.

Mr. Cooke marveled at the quality of the cotton. He picked up a handful from a bale, took in the fragrance, and analyzed the fullness of the boll. "Mrs. Moon, howeva do ya manage to harvest such high-quality cotton?" For years, the Magnolia Blossom Plantation always topped all the other plantation owners in Valdosta leaving her competitors taking second or third place after her father's crop.

"Well, I most certainly cannot tell y'all my family secret, now can I?"

Mr. Cooke went to the left side of the wagon and repeated his previous gestures, only to find the exact same quality. He even dug deep into another bale, hoping to find some low-quality cotton boll, but he was disappointed once again. "Please follow me, Mrs. Moon."

Just before she turned to follow Mr. Cooke, she winked at her two slaves. "Comin'."

Wesley watched his mistress attentively and was extremely amused by her attitude when dealing with these old slave-owners.

"Mrs. Moon, I can offer you five cents per pound." He began his song and dance.

Maggie Mae was very irritated and wanted to kick him in his family jewels, but she hid her emotions so as to get what she wanted from him. She poured out the honey. "Mr. Cooke, now you know very well that my cotton is worth at least ten cents per pound. Why, if I remember correctly, when daddy was alive, you paid him over ten cents a pound for our high quality cotton and now you wanna pay me half?" she pulled out her black, lace fan and began fanning herself while batting her eyes.

He found her irresistible, as he always did, even when she would join her father, paying close attention to the money exchanges. Then she grew into a young lady, and he never saw her again until her husband left for war. She was not only the most beautiful, available woman in town, she was an expert negotiator. He would have added, better than her own father. "Very well, six cents."

"Nine cents." Her smile stretched from ear to ear.

"Six and a half cents." He held steady.

"Mr. Cooke, I will take nothin' less than seven cents or I'm afraid I'll have to take this high-quality cotton to Atlanta, as I'm certain the English merchants will pay over ten cents for it." She continued to fan and bat her eyes.

She drove a hard bargain, but she was irresistible. "Very well, we have a deal. Seven cents." He stretched his hand and she gently shook it. **He** was the one who would get over ten cents from the English, not her. The English were very prejudiced against women running businesses. "Have your slaves bring the bales in, please." He opened the cash drawer and began pulling out bank notes.

Wesley and Charles began to unload the bales of cotton, being very careful not to rip the surrounding fabric, as very much was lost during the loading and unloading. They wanted their mistress to get as much as she could for this magnificent crop. Maggie Mae was very satisfied and smiled every time the men passed by. She tried to make sure that Wesley noticed that she was smiling at him, even though she pretended to be exchanging pleasantries with the other slaveowners. Many deep, loving looks were exchanged within those minutes.

After the men carried the last bale in, Mr. Steward stopped Wesley by grabbing his arm, in his return to the wagon to wait for his mistress. "Where you goin' Negro?"

Wesley grunted and looked fearfully at Maggie Mae.

"Why you lookin' at her, Negro, you best be lookin' at me."

Maggie Mae stormed up and got right in Mr. Steward's face, forcing him to let go of Wesley. "Sir, why are you harassin' my new slave? Why, he doesn't speak hardly any English, ya see he's only been here for less than a week." Then she turned to Wesley. "You go!" she pointed to the wagon.

With his head down, he fled to the wagon and climbed up along with Charles.

"In the future, Mr. Steward, I would be obliged if you address me and not my slaves," she demanded, holding her head high. She was not going to allow this scoundrel, who was always jealous of her father's crop and did everything he could to hinder any negotiations between them, to intimidate her—or her slaves.

"Well, I don't like the way he was starin' at ya. That ain't right." He was still peering at Wesley. There was something about that slave he didn't like.

"Mr. Steward, my new slave ain't never done this job, so he was concerned that he would mess it up. That's why he was lookin' at me; he was assurin' my approval." She was fuming but hid it very well. "Now, if you don't mind, my slaves have work to do." She was fearless and determined to get her way with these God-awful men. She headed to Mr. Cooke's desk and waited patiently until the two men had completed unloading the wagon. When the last bale was gently placed on the pile, she turned to Mr. Cooke and opened her small purse.

"Here you go, Mrs. Moon. Would ya mind countin' it? I wanna make sure I counted right." As he handed her the bills, he gently patted her hand.

She felt it even under her glove and got a shiver down her spine, but she acted as if nothing happened. She carefully counted her money. "It's all there."

"Very good. Please sign here." And again, he touched her as he handed her the pen.

She scribbled her signature and placed the pen on the notebook. She placed the cash in her purse, turned, and left the marketplace. "Good day, gentlemen." Charles was waiting for his mistress alongside the wagon to help her up. "To the bank, Charles."

Charles hurried to the driver side of the wagon, leaving Wesley in the bed. He had kept his head down throughout the ordeal, but heard every word that was said. He was beginning to understand why his grandfather loathed the south.

Just a few minutes passed, and they stopped right in front of the bank. "Now, y'all wait here."

"Yes'm." Charles replied as Wesley stayed silent.

As soon as Maggie disappeared inside the bank, Wesley asked, "Why did those men treat her so terribly?"

"Lower your voice, son." He looked around. "Dats cuz she a woman. Dem fools don't know what respect is." Then he giggled. "But missy Maggie sure got 'em fooled. Didn't ya notice her playin' 'em like a fiddle? Dat was sumpin' ta watch, it waz." He giggled some more.

Wesley was taken aback as he watched Maggie Mae stand up to those vipers. So much so, that he became aroused at the scene.

"All right, I'm headin' to the general store. Can y'all bring the wagon over?" It was only a few buildings away. She pulled out her fan and started fanning as she entered the store.

"Good mornin', Mrs. Moon. How y'all doin' today?" Mrs. Potters owned the store together with her husband.

"Oh, I'm just fine." She proceeded to look around.

"What can I help ya with today?"

"I need some cotton seed."

"I figured as much." She smiled falsely and waved Maggie Mae to follow her to the storeroom at the rear. "Did ya sell your crop?"

"Yes, ma'am I did."

"And they treated you well?" Mrs. Potters was a jealous viper, but she loved making money as much as the next slaveowner. She didn't have slaves of her own, as it was not proper for slaves to work behind the counter serving white folk. They were just not smart enough to handle money and merchandise properly.

"Oh, yes, very well."

"Oh good." Yes, of course it was good. Good for her store. Maggie Mae and her father always went to the Potters' general store right after they sold their crop at market. They knew that the seed the Potters sold was the best in the state. "Well, here it is. Shall I give you the usual amount?"

"Yes, of course." Maggie Mae knew well that Gwendolyn Potters was one of the most gossipy and vile women in the south and she also knew well to keep a good distance from her. Not to mention, withholding any information about her family situation that could trigger jealousy, envy, or even worse, seizure of her estate, especially since she was Mr. Hart's sister. She had decided after her beloved Roland died that her plantation would be inherited by her children if it was the last thing she did.

"Well, how are you managin' without your husband?"

"Quite fine. Quite fine, indeed." She took some of the seed in her hand and examined it just like her father taught her. "Very good quality, as always, Mrs. Potters." She knew the words to say to butter up that snake.

"Well, I do appreciate that." She gave her an extra scoop of seed as a reward for those kind words. It was only fair.

"Charles! Y'all come in and put this here seed on the wagon." She almost said please but she bit her tongue. Then she went back inside the store and looked around. She would have loved to buy some fabric, but she couldn't. She had Rose take apart her mother's outfits and turn them into the very latest fashions. There were so many different fabrics and styles that would keep Rose busy for years. Besides, she was still wearing mostly black, so there was no need for new fabrics, presently.

"What else can I get ya?"

Maggie Mae pulled out a list that Harriet had prepared for her. She was the eldest slave and was like a second mother to her. She knew exactly what was needed around the house. "There." She handed the list to Mrs. Potters.

Mrs. Potters took the list and looked at it with her beady brown eyes. Then she began to gather all the items on the list and place them in a crate that Wesley brought in. "I see ya got a new slave."

Maggie Mae didn't raise her head. "Yes, I did."

"Can yo afford one these days? Times are pretty hard."

"Yes, they are, but I needed a few more men to help with the land and other things only men can do."

"He looks different that the others. Where did you buy him from?"

"Atlanta." She wasn't going to give her any long and winded answers.

"Ah, I see." She put a few more items in the crate while Wesley and Charles waited outside. "He's very fit. Where's he from?"

"Oh, some African country called Nigeria, I believe," trying to make nothing of it.

"Ni-what?" Mrs. Potters finished loading the crate. "Nevamind. Here ya go."

"Charles! Have him come git this crate!"

"Doesn't he have a name?"

"Yes, but for the life of me, I caint remember it. I need to give him a Christian name, I s'pose." She watched as Wesley picked up the crate and took it to the wagon without raising his eyes from the floor. "So, how much do I owe ya, Mrs. Potters?"

"Well, let me see." She wrote the total on the same list that Maggie Mae gave her earlier.

"Is that with the seed?"

"Yes, ma'am."

Maggie Mae pulled out the exact amount from her purse and handed it to Mrs. Potters. "Good day, Mrs. Potters."

She pushed a few buttons on her cash register. A bell rang and the cash drawer opened. She carefully placed the cash in order and shut the drawer.

"Gwen, I'm home and I'm hungry." Mr. Potters exclaimed as he entered the store from the back door.

"Oh good, you're home." She untied her apron and handed it to her husband. "There's a little sumpin' on the stove for ya." She took her hat and her purse and headed out the front door.

"Why? Where ya headin'?"

"I'm gonna have a word with Mrs. Hart." As she closed the door, the bell clanged.

He shrugged and headed toward the kitchen.

Chapter Eleven

"That was really something." Wesley was finally able to break his supposed language barrier.

"Whatever do ya mean?"

"I mean you. Having to fight to get a good price on your cotton. And keeping up that story about me. You should become an actress."

"An actress? Well, I suppose that's a compliment."

"It is, indeed. I've never seen such acting and I've been to several plays up north."

"Well, Lieutenant, this acting is crucial to the livelihood of my family. I have no choice. If I seem weak, they will be on me like white on rice."

"Do ya understan' why we pretendin' to be ha slaves?"

"Yes, Charles, I do now." He took in the fresh, early evening air. "You know, I could probably get you more money for your cotton."

Maggie Mae's curiosity was piqued. "Just how do you think you could do that?"

"Well, President Lincoln gave licenses to traders who follow the Union army into the South. In fact, I know a few who are staying with another brigade settled just a few miles north of here."

"Tell me more."

"These Union agents are willing to pay the highest prices—or they offer badly needed supplies as barter."

"Huh. I see."

"Yes, and these agents also buy other types of crops, like tobacco, hemp, and flax."

"Flax? That's what is growing on the southeast end of the plantation."

"Yes, I noticed that."

"How do they pay?"

"In Union dollars, of course."

"Well, that money is useless to me. I need Confederate money right now so I can feed my family."

Wesley loved the way she called her slaves her "family". He felt her heart was in the right place.

"Yes but once we win the war, and we will, you can use it to buy whatever you'd like because it is most probable that the Confederate money will disappear, and be worthless, once the Union wins."

"Well, you certainly are most self-confident."

"Yes, ma'am, I am."

"All right then, I'll humor you. Can you get one of those agents to buy our flax?"

"I probably can."

"Well, all right then. The flax should be ready in a few weeks. I would be happy to meet with your agent then."

As they approached the house, Lizzy and Pauly came running out. Charles helped Maggie Mae down.

"Mama!"

"Did you sell your cotton, mama?"

"Yes, darlin', I did."

"Good." Pauly had stepped up to be the leader of the family since his father passed and he was a bit anxious about his mother going into town and selling the crop. He didn't think she could handle it, but he had to admit to himself that she could.

"Yo' mama wuz sumthin awesome, son. Why, she done played doze men like a fiddle, she did."

"Thank you, Charles. I was a little worried, there, too."

"No need. You were perfect." Wesley helped Charles and the children unload the wagon.

Maggie Mae could not help but smile in satisfaction of what she just heard. She was terrified when she confronted those men, but the thought of Wesley looking over her shoulders was a comfort. She was surely beginning to be more than fond of this Union soldier. "Chesney, what's for dinner?" she yelled as she entered the kitchen. "And where are we eatin'?"

"Evnin', Missy Maggie. I got dinner ready for ya and yo' young'ns in the dinin' room. The rest of us are eatin' on the back porch."

"No. I wanna eat with y'all. We are eatin' like a family tonight, and later on y'all are gonna get paid." She was enormously proud of her accomplishment and being able to have enough money to pay her workers. All the sacrifices she and her family have made is paying off. She was joyous and it clearly showed with every skip in her step and the smile that stretched from ear to ear.

Like a big, happy, colorless family, they ate; they drank; they chattered; and they sang. A couple of Yankees played a fiddle and a guitar. They merrily talked about all sorts of things like when they thought the war was going to end. What would happen to the South when it was over? Would all the slaves be freed? Would they be able to stay with their mistress? The younger children played and ran around the large dinner table while some of the

Yankees took them on their knees and told them stories, reminiscing of when they were telling those same stories to their own children. There was laughter and tears. Memories in the making.

After dinner, most of Wesley's men retired to their barracks, while Maggie Mae and Wesley had their dessert and coffee in the parlor. They chuckled and giggled. She lightly touched his arm and he patted her hand. They were becoming more and more friendly and confident with each other while Harriet observed with disdain and the fear of the scandal that was slowly forming right under her nose. As much as she gestured and sighed her disagreement, Maggie Mae was not picking up on her signals, and this was very disconcerting for Harriet. The day would soon come when she, as the slave matriarch, would have to lay down the Southern law of the white man.

~~~~~~

As Wesley was preparing for bed, as per his nightly ritual, he pulled out his Bible and read a few passages. Then he pulled out his grandmother Kanika's brooch. It was the only piece of jewelry his grandfather was able to give her, other than her wedding ring, which had been bequeathed to one of Wesley's cousins. He loved to take it out of its blue velvet pouch and admire it under the dim candlelight. He loved the way the many different colored stones shimmered and glowed. He had promised his grandfather that he would give it to the woman he loved. Suddenly Maggie Mae stepped into his thoughts. He imagined her wearing that brooch and how it would bring out her splendid eyes and her ivory skin. Ivory skin. What was he thinking? How could he even imagine a life with a southern belle—a white woman! No! He had to remove any thoughts of romance with that woman. It was taboo! He placed the brooch back into the pouch, closed the Bible and placed it on his lamp stand.

    Maggie Mae was also performing her bedtime ritual. She got out of her black dress and put on her cotton night gown, put her hair up in her nightcap, read a scripture passage, and kissed the image of her beloved Roland. As she stared at her husband's image, it slowly morphed into Lieutenant Jenkins, or Wesley as she had become more at ease with him. She thought about the comments made by Mrs. Potters. Maggie Mae had to agree with her. He was not your typical slave. He was well-built, with an air of nobility about him. He was gentle, kind, very well spoken, and black. Why did he have to be black? That was a forbidden color, and Lord only knows what they would do to her if they ever found out she was harboring a Yankee brigade—not to mention, they were all black.

Wesley couldn't sleep. His thoughts were continually racing towards Maggie Mae. Am I falling for her? What spell has she cast on me? Why can't I get her off my mind? He tossed and turned, but every time he closed his eyes, he saw her beautiful, porcelain, white face. Enough, already!

"There's no use!" he whispered to himself as he quietly got out of bed, put his trousers on, and headed out into the brisk night air. He stared at the full moon. He always wondered why it was that people's madness would come out with the full moon. Was the animal inside trying to escape? Somehow, he ended up pacing up and down right under Maggie Mae's window.

Maggie Mae was restless, and even after tossing and turning, she could not sleep. Her thoughts were drifting towards Wesley. The thought of his arms around her made her tingle with pleasure. What would it be like to kiss him? What would it be like to caress his face? What would it be like to touch that hard and muscular body? What would it be like to make love with him? So many questions! She was already uncovered but she felt like she was working the land with the plough; something she had not done since she was a child. She couldn't take it anymore, so she got up and put on her robe. She didn't light the oil lamp because the full moon was beaming through her window, lighting up the entire room. She went to the window to open it up. Lo and behold, Wesley was pacing up and down right in front of her bedroom.

"What on earth is he doing there?" she whispered to herself.

Wesley felt eyes on him, so he looked up at her with a desiring look.

She stuck her head out the window and waved.

He motioned her to come down.

Maggie Mae could not help but heed his command. She rushed out of her bedroom and headed out the side door, being as quiet as a mouse. She ran into his open arms and they kissed passionately. She melted in his arms. She knew that was what was keeping her awake. They parted.

"This is wrong! This is so wrong!"

"No, Wesley, I disagree." She gently patted his face with her soft, trembling hand.

His hands grasped both her arms to keep her at a distance. With a tremor in his voice, he spoke. "Maggie Mae, I know this is wrong, terribly wrong, but I love you. I've loved you since the first time I laid eyes on you...but...I'm black...and you're...your skin...is like porcelain...I...I..." he pressed his lips on hers so hard he almost felt his lips explode.

They fell to the damp, soft ground, still wound up together. The passion was intense. He towered over her, looking into her honest, blue eyes, full of unspoken love, with his lips gently brushing hers, sending shivers down her spine and making her tremble.

"If you want me to stop, do it now, because I cannot hold back any longer, my love..."

She pulled off her nightgown, pulled him down to her, and kissed him gently—which slowly turned into want. She relieved him of his nightshirt, while his mouth was all over her body. He groaned softly, low in his throat, and then his arms encircled her, gathering her against him, as they became entangled together, still kissing. It seemed that they couldn't stop. His hands ran slowly up into her curly dark hair, shimmering in the moonlight, and then down over her delicate shoulders and along her arms.

"Oh, Wesley! Wesley! Darling!" she cried out into the night holding his lean, muscular male body against hers.

"My Maggie...I love you...I ache for you...but this is wrong...so wrong...we can't...we mustn't..." he lifted himself on top of her as if he was floating over her.

"I don't care, Wesley, I love you too. I'm not afraid, because it's not wrong. How can love be wrong?" she looked into his fearful eyes showing only passion and desire. "Please, take me now, I'm yours!" she pulled him down again, pressing her throbbing lips against his.

This time he did not hesitate. He entered her slowly, thrusting deeply, and then off into a reckless abandon. Maggie Mae let out a cry of passion. As his rhythm accelerated, her desire for him soared.

From over yonder, behind one of the slave-house windows, a terribly upset and astonished Harriet was watching, while tears streamed down her face.

Chapter Twelve

Maggie Mae felt like she was floating above the clouds, but the same time, sloshing in the mire. It was now a year since Roland's passing and she was in love again. She never thought she could love again, at all—much less, a handsome, strongly-built black man. But she did. She picked up her husband's photograph, looked at it with loving eyes, and frowned. A wave of guilt flooded her psyche. "I know you would not approve of this, my love, but you're not here anymore and he is. I still miss you so, but my heart is beating again. I'm so sorry, my love." She put the photograph back in its place, face down.

"Did ya call me, Missy Maggie?" Flora opened Maggie Mae's door.

"Well, no, but now that you're here, I'll get up."

Flora headed to the armoire and, as she had been doing for the past year, she pulled out the mourning garb.

"No, Flora, no. I'm dun wearin' black. I want color."

Flora stopped in her tracks. "Are you sure, Maggie?"

"Yes I am. Today is the one-year anniversary of Roland's death."

"A year? Well, my goodness, time done fly by so fast."

"Sure has." She headed towards the armoire. She went through the clothing and pulled out a burgundy colored cotton dress that belonged to her mother and then tailored by Rose to perfection for Maggie Mae's figure. "My, my, Rose sure did a wonderful job on mama's dress! Don'tcha think?"

"Yes'm, she got golden hands, she does."

"Well, all right. I shall wear this one today."

"Are ya going somewhere?"

"Yes, I am. Wes—uh, Lieutenant Jenkins is going to introduce me to a buyer for the flax. Seems like I can get more money for it than at the Valdosta market."

"Is dat right?" she started to prepare a tub of warm water for her mistress.

"Yes, indeed." She had stripped naked and was almost ready to climb into the tub. "Hurry, Flora! I'm chilly!"

"Yes, Maggie." She scurried down the stairs to fetch more hot water that was boiling on the stove. "Be right there!" she yelled towards the back staircase.

"Whatcha yellin' 'bout?" Harriet was finishing up breakfast for the men gathered on the back porch.

"I'm fetchin' water for Maggie." She lifted the heavy pitcher.

"Huh, ya better scrub her good…" she mumbled under her breath.

Flora ignored her comments since she didn't really hear them, not to mention the fact that she wasn't very fond of Harriet, anyway. She expertly climbed the stairs and entered Maggie Mae's room again without spilling a drop of water. She poured the water into the tub as her mistress climbed in.

"Ah, this is nice."

As per usual, she picked up the bar of soap that Harriet had made, and using a linen facecloth, Flora began scrubbing.

Maggie Mae crinkled her nose. "My goodness, that soap smells awful bad."

"I know, I know, but we can't afford no soap from that there France."

"Awww, how I wish I had some, though. I do miss it; indeed, I do."

"Well, I thought you liked Harriet's soap?"

"I did while I was in mourning, and I ain't no more. A woman just can't smell like this here soap." She cringed at the sight of it. "I'm gonna buy me one of them nice smelly soaps next time I go to the Potters' Store."

"Well, I suppose one bar ain't gonna do no harm."

"Missy Maggie, Lieutenant Wesley iz 'ere!" Charles yelled from the bottom of the stairs.

"Comin'."

Wesley had entered the kitchen door with a shorter, stout, white man wearing round spectacles and dressed handsomely. "Mrs. Moon, this is Mr. Banner."

"So very nice to make yar acquaintance, Mr. Banner."

"Likewise, Mrs. Moon." He was astonished at the beauty of this southern Belle. He very lightly kissed the back of her hand.

A spark of jealousy seeped into Wesley, but he knew he had nothing to worry about. "Shall we go to the barn?"

"Yes, Lieutenant. This way please." Maggie Mae swooshed by them and led them out to the barn. Upon their arrival at the barn, she opened the large doors and stepped in. "Here we are."

The barn was rather unremarkable, though it smelled of a mixture of somewhat fresh paint, horse droppings, and the clean, crisp, and slightly nutty fragrance of the flax.

Mr. Banner didn't hesitate to remove a handful of flax and bring it to the early afternoon light, examining it attentively. Then he grabbed another handful and repeated his actions. He did this several more times, until he was satisfied with his examination. "Mrs. Moon, I must say, I have never seen flax like this. You must have a secret."

Maggie Mae smiled with much satisfaction. "I certainly do," was all she said. She didn't know this man, so she limited her words, the words of her father: "Maggie Mae, always remember, a man of knowledge restrains his words. Always leave them wanting just a little bit more."

Mr. Banner pulled out a small leather-bound notebook. "Enough said. Mrs. Moon I am willing to offer you two hundred and seventy-five dollars for this crop."

Wesley looked at Maggie Mae, raising his eyebrows while she smiled with satisfaction.

"Three hundred even."

"You're killing me! How can I make any money at that price? I'm already going to lose money when I go to resell!"

"Mr. Banner, I know full well that you will be able to sell this crop for four hundred and seventy-five dollars, up north. I have expenses, too, you know. I'm sure you will not want this to be a wasted trip, now. Am I right?"

"All right. Ma'am, you drive a hard bargain. Where did you learn to negotiate like that?"

"Never you mind. Just accept this deal or high tail it out of my sight, because I have work to get done."

Mr. Banner shook her hand. "All right. It's a deal."

"Mr. Banner, if I may, how will you be paying me?"

"In Union dollars, of course."

"I see. Well, do you have any Confederate money?"

He pulled out a large black leather portfolio, opened it, and searched for the southern currency. "Yes, yes…I have twenty dollars…would that work for you, Mrs. Moon?"

It was not a lot, but it would buy her some staples for the plantation. "Yes, that will do just fine."

He pulled the cash out, counted the Confederate dollars, placing them in one neat pile. Then he counted the Union dollars, placing them in another parallel pile. "Here you are, three hundred dollars, twenty of which are Confederate bills."

"Oh, thank you Mr. Banner. Would you like to stay for tea?"

"Oh, I would be delighted, but I'd best be going. It is quite dangerous for me to be seen around these parts." He bowed and placed his black silk hat on his head. "Good day, Mrs. Moon. I hope to see you again soon."

"Same here." She waved. "Please be safe."

"I will." And he disappeared down over the hill.

~~~~~~

Several weeks later, Maggie Mae and Wesley were sitting on the porch in the rocking chairs, and chit-chatting. They had become inseparable since that night, and there have been several intimate encounters since then. All in secret and all in quiet solitude. Wesley was looking out at the horizon when he saw some clouds of dust rising from the dirt road at the end of the plantation. He got up and placed his hand on his forehead to shield his eyes from the sun's glare.

"What is it?" she asked as she got up, as well, to look.

"Seems to me like someone is heading this way."

"Yes, I think you're right." She suddenly became angry. "And I know who it is." She opened the side door and quickly headed inside. "Y'all, go and get your daddies. We got company and they ain't friendly. Now git!" She headed back to the porch. "Wesley, go get as many of your men as possible and get them out of their uniforms."

"Who are they, Maggie?"

"The Harts. And they ain't nice folk, I assure ya. Now git!"

Wesley took off to the barracks as fast as he could. "Men! Fall in! Grab your weapons. No uniforms!" The men quickly shed their uniforms and got into plain clothes. He, too, picked up his rifle and headed toward the house.

Maggie was now standing on the front porch with Charles by her side. "Y'all remember our plan?" As per the plan, anyone who had been taught to handle a gun, aside from the Yankee soldiers, were to hide in the side bushes, ready to pounce. All the women and younger children, including Lizzie and Pauly, gathered in the kitchen, hovering together. Harriet assured them that they were not in danger. But they had to stay close together in case anything happened.

"Who are they?" asked Sergeant Blackwell.

"The Harts."

"What do they want?"

"They want my plantation."

"Why?"

"Dey is evil folk, dey is." Charles shook his head.

The Harts didn't seem to be the only ones in the group. There were at least another half dozen following the Hart coach, and they were approaching quickly.

"Why do they want your plantation? Is there a lien on it?"

"Absolutely not! My daddy owned every inch and he bought it piece by piece. They never liked my daddy 'cause he was nice to the slaves. My daddy's crops were always the best quality and he always got top dollar at the market. Those snakes never understood why our crops were the best in southern Georgia."

The angry caravan was only about a half mile away. "My men are ready, and we won't let anything happen to your plantation."

"Well, best be ready for wah, son, cuz dats what I'm feelin'."

The first coach to stop in front of the house was Hart's, and all the rest stopped behind his. Ben Hart was the first to descend from his coach with his son, James right behind him. He tipped his hat and smiled deviously at Maggie Mae. Then, one by one, from the rest of the coaches, several men exited and headed to where Ben was standing. There were armed men in Confederate uniforms, there were men from the marketplace, and there were men dressed up in their Sunday best, like politicians.

"Mrs. Moon. I have come here today to give you one more chance to sell your plantation. To me." He pulled out a piece of paper. "This here is the contract drawn up by Mr. Gable, himself." He stepped forward and handed the document to Maggie Mae.

"I see." She took it and began reading.

"As you can see, it is a generous offer."

She took her sweet time in reading the document, allowing Wesley's men to set up in a strategic position.

"Well, Mrs. Moon, do we have a deal?"

Maggie Mae tore the document in half and in half again, right under Ben Hart's nose. She tossed the torn pages, which flew away with the light breeze. "Does that answer your question, Mr. Hart?" she gave him a self-satisfied smile.

"Mrs. Moon, I would strongly recommend that you take my offer…"

"Or else?"

"Or else, it will be taken from you."

She pulled out her father's pistol from inside her bosom and pointed it at Ben. "And by whom, may I ask?"

Ben raised his hands in the air. "Mrs. Moon, now be reasonable. You are the only white woman in the Confederacy runnin' a plantation. You cannot possibly continue. Women can never be plantation owners or slave owners." He was trying to be as calm as he could, but her stubbornness was irritating him.

Her finger was gently stroking the trigger. Oh, how she wanted to put that man out of her misery. "Mr. Hart, have you looked around? Does it really look like I can't handle this plantation?"

He had no intention of taking his eyes off the pistol, still pointed directly at his head. "No, I have not. I don't need to."

"Well, don't bother. I assure you that I'm handling MY plantation just fine."

"Please Mrs. Moon, don't make this harder than it needs to be."

"Mr. Hart, I suggest you take your men and leave MY plantation, this instant…" she whistled. "Or else, I cannot be held responsible for what might happen next."

The number of black men armed with rifles that suddenly appeared out of the bushes and all pointing their weapons towards the caravan, outnumbered them two to one.

"Mrs. Moon, on behalf of your Democrat Party, I demand you order your slaves to lower their weapons before they get hurt."

"Mr. Mayor, I don't care what the Democrat Party has to say. This is MY plantation that MY daddy left to ME." And she pointed the gun in his direction.

The Mayor also raised his hands. "Mrs. Moon, don't you understand that only a man is allowed to own a plantation?"

"Is that right? Who says?"

"Why, it's written in the Constitution of the Confederacy."

"Mr. Mayor, I assure you that what you are declarin' is not in the Constitution, believe me."

Taken aback, he asked: "How do you know this?"

"I read it. Pure and simple. You see, Mr. Mayor, while my slaves are working the land of this here

Magnolia Blossom Plantation, I am home-schoolin' my children."

The Mayor and Ben were both silent, since they didn't know what was written in the Constitution. Neither of them had ever read it. They both looked at each other with much doubt in their eyes. There was nobody there who could confirm what she just said.

"If I may, I'd like you to hear what IS in the Constitution: A well-regulated militia being necessary to the security of a free State, the right of the people to keep and bear Arms, shall NOT be infringed."

The silence was deafening. The men had nothing to say after this Southern Belle let them have it with both barrels! Wesley was amused, to say the least, and he was aroused by her courage, fearlessness, and intelligence.

"Now, y'all need ta leave before I give the command to start shootin'!"

"This is NOT over!" Ben yelled as he turned and climbed up on his coach.

"Yes, it is, Mr. Hart, yes, it is! And if any of y'all come 'round here again, I'll make sure ya leave feet first. Ya hear? Now, get the hell out! And don't come back!"

None of the black men made a move until the caravan was long out of their sight and the dust had settled.

As Wesley took a sigh of relief, Maggie Mae collapsed to the floor.

"Miss Maggie, Miss Maggie?" Charles knelt next to her, took her hand, and patted it.

Wesley ran up to Maggie and took her in his arms. "Open the door! I'll take her up to her room." As he walked in and headed up the stairs, Flora and Harriet were right behind. Flora went ahead of him and opened her mistress's door. Harriet had her lips tightened and was shaking her head. He laid her gently on her bed.

"What could be wrong with her?" he was terrified.

Harriet grabbed him by his shoulders and pushed him towards the door. "Son, this ain't none of yo' bizness. Git out! Git!"

"But I wanna…"

"I said, GIT!"

He left, frowning, as Flora closed the door behind him.

"Mammy, whaz goin' on?"

Harriet lifted Maggie Mae's petticoat. "Dis is whaz goin' on. She dun lost her babi!" there was a huge bloodstain right in the middle.

"A babi? Maggie was wit child?" she was incredulous.

"Yes'm."

"B-but how? When? Who?" then the look on her face was showing what just entered her mind.

"Wesley!" they said, in unison.

Chapter Thirteen

"But why can't I see her?"

"Cuz yo' is a Negro, and Negros cain't go in white folks' rooms. I don' no how y'all do it up Nawth, but around these parts it jus' ain't allowed." Charles was trying to keep him from going upstairs and seeing his mistress. He could not allow that, especially now that he knew what was going on. He stood on the bottom step of the staircase. "Now, git."

"At least tell me if she's all right. I need to know. Please?"

"She fine. Dat Missa Hart dun upset her real bad. She needs rest, is all."

For some odd reason, he didn't believe Charles, but if he fought him, he would have had another hornets nest on his hands. "Fine. I will go. But please, if anything changes, I want to know."

Charles said nothing. He only nodded. He was on the same page as his wife on this one.

With his proverbial tail between his legs, Wesley left the house and went back to the barracks. He felt he was missing something but could not quite put his finger on it. He was not giving up though. On the contrary, this was not over.

~~~~~~

"I-I need to get up." Maggie Mae tried to sit up, but her head spun around. She groaned and lay back down.

"No, ya don't! Ya need ta rest, ya hear?" Harriet scolded her.

"What happened, Mammy?" still feeling groggy.

"Uh girl, you dun causin' trouble, you is." Harriet had a stern look of disapproval on her face.

"Whatta ya mean, Mammy?" she knew Harriet well, and suspected that she knew more than she was saying.

Harriet sighed. "I'm ashamed of ya! So, ashamed." She walked out the door.

"But Mammy, what did I do? Mammy!"

Flora flew upstairs when she heard Maggie Mae yell.

"Mammy?"

"No, it's me."

"Flora, what is with mammy?"

"Well…I…"

"Flora, I want the truth, now!"

"All right, all right, now don't be mad, Maggie."

"I will be mad until someone tells me what's goin' on? Why am I in bed and why am I feelin' so weak?"

Flora fluffed up Maggie Mae's pillows and added a couple more so she could sit up a bit. "Well, seems you fainted right after that evil man left."

"I did?"

"Yes'm."

"I see, so this is why I'm in bed?"

"Yes'm."

"Go on."

Flora took a deep breath. "You lost the baby."

Maggie Mae's eyes popped out of her head. "What baby? What on earth are you talking about?"

"Missy Maggie, you waz with chile."

"With child?"

"Yes'm."

"…was…you mean…"

Flora picked up the dirty petticoat from the basket and showed Maggie Mae the stain.

"Ah, I see." Tears welled in her eyes. "Wesley." She muttered.

"Ya wanna see him? I can…"

"No Flora, that's all right." She turned over to the other side of the bed facing the window. "I'd like to be alone now."

Flora picked up the basket of Maggie Mae's dirty clothes and left the room.

The next morning, Maggie Mae got up slowly, put her robe on, and sluggishly went to the kitchen to have some breakfast.

"Mornin' Missy Maggie! How ya feelin'?" Harriet poured a cup of coffee for her mistress.

"Oh, all right, I guess." Truth be known, she didn't really know how she was feeling. Physically she was still a bit weak, but, also, she was deeply hurt by the loss of her baby and of her lover. She had to face the fact that this love of hers was prohibited by the law of the land and it was just plain wrong. A white woman simply cannot love a black man. *Perhaps God did this, for my own good.*

"What are ya up ta eatin'?"

"Whatever ya have ready is fine."

"All right, how 'bout sum porridge?"

"Maggie Mae, ya feelin' betta?"

"Yes, Mammy, I am." She started picking at her porridge.

Harriet motioned for Chesney to leave the kitchen. She didn't need to be told twice. She was out of sight in a flash. Harriet sat down right across from Maggie Mae.

"Mmm…mmm…mmm…what did you dun?"

Maggie Mae teared up. "Mammy, I'm sorry…"

"Missy Maggie, ya know I luv ya like yo' is one of my own. So, I'm gonna take yo' mamma's place right now, cuz I know ya needs a mamma."

Maggie Mae dried her sniffles.

"What waz ya thinkin' chile? Sleeping with a Negro! It ain't ra't, just ain't ra't!"

"I know Mammy, but what am I to do? I love him and I don't care what color he is. I love him very much, and I cain't go back now, I just cain't."

"Ya gots ta, child! Ya cain't be seen wid no Negro man. And ta make t'ings worse, he's a Yankee…dis ain't ra't!"

"I know it ain't, but I think it's too late now, I love him and if I hadn't lost my baby, we'd be expectin' a child."

"No, honey chile, no! I fear for ya!" She got up and started pacing. "Those evil white men from the otha day, they's gonna com 'round ag'in and day gonn' tar an' featha ya! Day gonn' kill you! Den day gonn' kill all of us, send yo' chirrun ta sum o'phanage. Is dat what ya want?"

"Of course not."

"Den ya need ta stop. Ra't now. Stop dis madness affo' it's too late, ya heah?"

Maggie Mae got up, nodded, and went back upstairs.

"Ya best be heedin' what I said, chile!" Harriet yelled from the bottom of the stairs. Shaking her head, she went to join Charles in the front garden.

"Did ya talk to her?"

"Lawd, I tried. Lawd knows I tried."

"Well, what she say?"

"Seems like she loves him."

"Love? Ain't no white woman evva luved a Negro. She dun lost her san'ty." Angrily, he grabbed a handful of weeds from the flower bed, pulled them from the ground, and tossed them to the wind.

"I heah ya. I'm terrified. This heah scandal can git us all killed and dis heah plantation, is gonna go straight to the evil Mista Hart. Oh, Massa George and Missy Anita is both rollin' in d'em graves, dey is."

"Now, Mammy, she ain't dumb. She know what's in store fo' her if dis gits out. Das big danger, big danger. I know she know dat."

"I sure hope so, fo' all our sakes. Lawdy Jesus, please, take care of dis here woman!" she exclaimed.

"I'm gonn' talk to the Yankee later on." He pulled some more weeds. It was therapeutic for him at this point.

"Gud idea. I is hopin' he'll heed our words."

~~~~~~

Wesley heard a light knock on his door. It was late but he was not sleeping. He couldn't. He got up and opened the door.

Charles removed his hat, nodded, and entered.

"What brings you here?"

"I is here to talk to ya, boy."

"Is Mag…I mean Mrs. Moon all right?"

Charles peered at him. He caught him almost calling her by first name. This can only mean one thing. "Boy, ya gots ta leave."

"What? Why?" he was taken aback by his statement.

"Cuz, whatcha doin' ain't right. Iz danger, 'tiz."

"Danger? What makes you say that?"

"Lookee 'ere, I know what you dun with Missy Maggie Mae an' I ain't da only one who knows."

Wesley frowned and sat down, hanging his head in shame. He paused to think. "What now?"

"Ya gots ta leave."

"Leave. But I can't. I have my troop to take care of. I can't leave."

"Now, ya listen to me, boy! Ya caint be doin' what yo' is, with Missy Maggie. Yo' is puttin' her in turrible danger. Turrible danger!"

"I realize that, but…"

"No, ya don't! Yo' a Yankee. Ya cain't imagine w'atz goin' on in dis heah south." He moved closer to Wesley, but he did not sit. "Do ya understand whaz gonna happen to Missie Maggie if them white folk find out she's havin' an affair with you? A Negro? A Yankee Negro at that! Why, they'll take her, probably tar an' feather her, take her land, her house, put her churrin' in an orphanage! Did ya even think 'bout dat?"

Wesley shook his head. "No, I didn't think about that."

"Den dey will take all of us an' kill us. Dey is mean folk, dey is. Really mean folk. Dey got no God, no dey don't."

"But I can't just leave, sir. I am the Lieutenant of this brigade and I must lead them."

"Den yo' gotz to lead dem ra't off dis plantation. Ya gots ta leave. Do ya wanna put Missie Maggie in danger? Do ya? Wut 'bout us? Ya wan' 'em ta kill us? Cuz dat's what they iz gon' do."

"Of course not."

"Well, then there aint nothin' mo ta say. Ya gotz ta go."

"Sir, if I may. Do you understand that if we leave, Mrs. Moon will be left vulnerable to those evil men that came here the other day? She and you will not be able to fend them off. As soon as we leave, they will come right back here, guns blazing, and take everything from her. I will not let that happen!"

Charles had nothing to say. Wesley was right, and he knew it. They were between a rock and a hard place. He knew very well that Mr. Hart would take advantage of her being alone and outnumbered. He thought of a solution while he wrung his straw hat in his hands.

"So, here's what I'm going to do." He got up and began pacing around. "I'm going to take half of my men with me. We're going into Florida and push the rebels further south."

"Wut 'bout da rest of 'em?"

"I'll leave them here…to protect you…to protect…mag—I mean Mrs. Moon."

"Well, I dunno nuttin' 'bout war, but any help we can git to fend off d'ose evil men is fine, fine indeed." He got up and headed for the door. "When you leavin'?"

"Tomorrow." He looked outside to see if it was clear before he let Charles leave. "Good night, sir."

"Nite, boy." And he disappeared into the darkness of the night.

Wesley did not return to sleep; instead he made his plans to leave Valdosta and head into Florida. He prepared a communique to be sent first thing in the morning. He paced up and down some more and made some coffee, while he continued to formulate his plans. His attention was drawn to something glimmering outside. He got up from his desk and peered into the night. He noticed that the glimmer was coming from the main house. Maggie Mae's bedroom window. He dropped everything, picked up his rifle, and headed out the door. After he was sure no one was around, he quickly moved toward her bedroom window.

Maggie Mae was about to turn off the light and lie down, when she heard something hitting her window. She got up, picked up her father's revolver that was sitting on her nightstand, and went to the window. Before opening it, she tried to see if there was any movement. But there was no moon and the night was very dark. She opened the window, pointed the gun toward the ground, and shouted. "Who goes there?" Her heart was pounding.

"Maggie, it's me. Wesley."

"Wesley!" she was relieved. "What are you doing here?"

"I need to see you! I have been worried sick. How are you?"

"Shhhh! I'm coming down." She shut the window. With her revolver in hand, she ran downstairs to open the kitchen door. She waved at him to come in.

He came in, swiftly, and took her in his arms. "Oh, my Lord, I've missed you so!" His eyes filled with moisture as he held her tightly.

"So have I." she caressed his face and kissed him passionately. "Come…" she pulled him.

"No." he knew well where she was leading him, but he remembered the conversation he'd just had with Charles.

"Why?" she was confused.

"Because…I…I…"

"I was with child," she blurted out. She felt she owed him an explanation.

"Wha-what?"

She gripped his face, fingers on one cheek and thumb on the other. She held his face so that they were eye-to-eye. She said it slower and a bit louder. "I was with child."

He had no words. Now he understood Charles's scorn. Now he understood the fear emanating from the old man. Now he understood why Charles begged him to leave.

"Please, say somethin'."

"I'm sorry. I'm so sorry. I should not have put you in this terrible situation." He fell to his knees. "Can you ever forgive me?" his voice broke.

She pulled his head to her bosom. "My darlin', you have nothing to be sorry about. I love you; don't you understand?"

"I – I don't deserve you. You cannot love me. You can't…you can't…" he wept hysterically.

She was tearful. Never did she see a man cry. She didn't know what to do. She simply held him tight until he was ready to talk.

"I put you in danger. I put everyone in danger. I'm a menace," he murmured among his sobs.

"Whatever do you mean?"

He got up and grabbed her shoulders. "Don't you see? I put you in grave danger by making love to you."

"But why?"

"Let me ask you this. What if that child had been born?"

She tilted her head. "I never thought of that."

"This is all my fault. I should have not taken advantage of you. I put you, your family, and your plantation in grave peril."

"No! You didn't. I never knew I was expectin' and even if I did, I would have never told anyone about our child. Why I probably would'a had Flora raise it."

"Well, this is not gonna happen again." He let her go. "I'm leaving in the morning." He turned towards the door.

"Leavin'?" she pulled his shirt. "You can't leave! I need you, Wesley! I need you!" she was shaking.

"I have to leave. I can't put you in this situation ever again."

"Please!"

"I must." He kissed her goodbye in a fiery way. Then he reached into his vest pocket and pulled out his grandmother's brooch. "Please keep this for me. No, it's yours."

Maggie Mae saw something shimmering under the faint candlelight. "Wesley, I couldn't." she slipped it back into his hand.

"Yes. It was my grandmother's." he held it up. "It was the only valuable piece of jewelry my grandfather was able to give her. Please, my love, take it. It's yours." Once again, he placed the brooch in her hand and gently folded her fingers around it.

She held it firmly against her heart. "I'll hold it for you. ***BUT.*** I want you to come back to me. Promise me!"

"Darling, I simply cannot make a promise I cannot keep."

"Wesley, please don't leave. What am I going to do without you?"

"Goodbye, Maggie." He kissed her forehead, hoisted his rifle over his shoulder, opened the door, and hurried back to his quarters, trying not to look back.

"But I love you," she whispered into the night breeze.

Chapter Fourteen

Pauly rushed into the kitchen. "Mama, where is Lieutenant Jenkins?"

Maggie Mae looked at her handsome young son. Tears welled in her eyes, but she had to contain her emotions. "He left, darlin'. He had to go fight down in Florida."

"Florida? Why on earth for?" he had grown very fond of Wesley.

"Yes, Mama, why did he leave?" Lizzy too, had become very close to the handsome Lieutenant.

She pulled both her children close to her. "Y'all must understand that he was not here permanently; he was just passin' through. He was ordered to go off to war."

"Oh, Mama, that is so unfair!"

"I know, my sweet boy, I know." She ruffled his hair. "Now, go on, go help with the farmin'. Go on."

"What about me, Mama?"

"Well, today, you're gonna do some needlepoint."

"Awww but Mama, I wanna help with the farmin' too."

"No, Lizzie, you're a young lady and you need to learn how to be one and act like one. Ya heah? Now go."

Lizzie folded her arms and tapped her left foot on the floor. But when her mother gave her the look, she grabbed her needlepoint ring and took off running toward the parlor.

"She sho' iz gittin' big."

"I know, Chesnee, I know. Frankly, it saddens me how time is flyin' by so quick."

Chesnee began cutting up vegetables. "Did he really leave?"

She couldn't look up. "Yes, he did. He's gone." Maggie Mae got up and put on an apron.

"Missy Maggie, can I say sumpin?"

"Of course, you can. You're family."

"I heard you was carryin' his child."

Maggie's lump didn't allow her to respond so she simply nodded.

"Well, I'm sorry. It'z always a sad day when a child iz called by our Lord."

She still couldn't muster any words. Again, she nodded.

"I s'pose itz for da best. Lord know wut he;z doin', He duz."

Maggie Mae dropped the knife and ran up the stairs to her room while tears streamed down her face.

Chesnee frowned. "Oh, my lands! Chesnee you dumma than a mud fence, you iz." Shaking her head.

~~~~~~

The end of August came around and the flax was harvested, awaiting a buyer. For the fear of not finding a buyer for her flax in town, Maggie Mae had decided to sell it to the Union buyer. Just like Wesley had promised her, he paid her top dollar and the dollars were Union dollars. Just like she did last time, she gathered her family together and distributed their earnings. Then she counted the rest and hid it under the rug in the parlor. Her father had dug out a small space where he stored his valuables and showed only Maggie Mae where it was and how to get into it. It was so well disguised and discreet that even if uncovered, you could not tell that the floor was cut out revealing the secret compartment. She pulled out the heavy metal box, opened it, and placed the money inside in a neat and tidy way. Then she pulled out Wesley's brooch, enjoying the luster one more time, wrapped it in her mother's favorite handkerchief, and gently placed it inside the box. She placed the metal box back in its place, replaced the wooden puzzle piece and covered it with the Turkish rug once again. The intention was to spend it when the United States were again united.

"It will happen." She whispered confidently.

Later that night, around two in the morning, Maggie Mae heard some stirring outside. She shot out of bed, pulled out the revolver from the nightstand, and ran down the stairs—so quickly, that she almost tumbled down. Charles was sleeping on a cot set up next to the kitchen door. "Charles, Charles!" she whispered as she shook him to awaken him.

"Huh? Wut?" he said groggily.

"Someone's out there."

He got up and went to look out the window. "I don't see nuttin'."

"Well, I tell ya, I heard something. Hurry, gather the men."

Charles picked up his rifle and the large bell that was to be rung as the signal for an emergency. He ran out into the night and rang the bell, looking around. It only took a minute or two for the Yankee soldiers to be ready, rifles in hand, whereas the older black children and the adults took a few more minutes to get ready.

As the clouds moved away, clearing the full moon to provide some decent light, everyone was in position.

Maggie Mae was just inside, in the hallway, peering out the window when she saw them. They were all standing about a hundred yards from the front door, aligned from left to right. She counted about fifty of them. Charles and Jonas joined her, clenching their rifles.

"Watz goin' on, Missy Maggie?" Jonas asked.

"Look for yourself…"

Jonas gently moved the filet curtain and looked out. Once again, the clouds cleared and the brilliant moon captured the night. It was the same group of men that attacked a few months back. "Oh, my, they is lots. I is countin' 'bout fitty."

"Are the soldiers in place?"

"Yes'm, Missy Maggie, just as we dun practice."

"What should I do, Charles?" she was truly missing Wesley right about now. "Should I go out there?"

"Well, Missy Maggie, as the matriarch of dis 'ere house, ya needs ta go confront 'em. Dey won't shoot a woman."

Maggie Mae thought about it for a few seconds. "Well, all right. Fanny, please to get the lantern."

Fanny ran to the kitchen, got the lantern, and turned the wheel to make the light brighter. She handed it to Maggie Mae. "Pleaz Missy Maggie, be careful. We is los' widout ya."

Maggie Mae nodded, took the lantern, took a deep breath and stepped out on the porch. "What do y'all want? Why are you here?"

"Mrs. Moon, you have played slaveowner for a long time now. Y'all need to let real men take over your plantation."

She recognized Benjamin Hart's voice.

"I most certainly will not!"

"Please, Mrs. Moon, you best be reasonable now. Please, I beg you, marry me and we can manage this here plantation together," James Hart begged. He had always desired her. He wanted to convince her the right way. There was no other woman who fired his passion up like she did. He had to have her; one way or another.

A shiver went down her spine. The day she married James would indeed be when hell freezes over. But she saw the dozens of guns pointing at her. "James Hart, is that you? Well, is that any way to ask for my hand in marriage?"

"Ummm…uh…I'm not…"

"Come closer, James, so we can talk."

As he began walking towards her, the clouds closed in and partially blocked the moonshine. "Maggie Mae…"

"James, come closer...now." She didn't move a muscle.

He moved to be only two feet away from her. She was standing on her porch and he was at the bottom of the two steps. She looked like a goddess in her thin, white night gown that revealed her perfect figure. He felt a sudden twitch of his masculinity.

"Good. Now, what was your question?"

"Well...I...want you to marry me. I want to be your husband and help you manage this here plantation."

"Is that so?"

"Yes, yes, I promise I'll be a good husband to ya, even better than Roland."

Maggie Mae's blood was boiling but she kept a straight face. She thought about her dear Roland. She hoped he did not hear what this vile man was promising her. *How dare he? Why he couldn't even hold a candle to Roland.* Not now, not ever! She descended one step. "Mr. Hart, I do appreciate your good intentions. But hear this. I will never, ever marry you. Not even if you were the last man in Valdosta. Do you understand me?"

Although he was steaming from rage, he nodded.

"Good. Now, go back to your snake in the grass of a father and leave my property immediately. Ya hear me?" she stepped back up backwards and moved slowly towards the door: one hand on the doorknob behind her and the other clutching the revolver inside her bosom.

James did an about face and marched back to his father's side. He whispered something in his father's ear. Benjamin's countenance turned extremely dour. He pulled out his shiny revolver with ivory grips and pointed it at her.

"Mrs. Moon, you leave me no choice."

"That is correct, Mr. Hart, you only have one choice and that is to leave my property immediately. Otherwise, we will begin to defend ourselves."

On that note, multiple clicks of weapons being cocked and readied rang into the night.

"I have a court order that gives me authorization to take your plantation." He waved the document so she could see it.

"Ha! That's rich, comin' from you! That's a fake paper and you know it! I will never give up my land, NEVER! Now, go on! Git! You have been warned." She turned the doorknob and slipped inside. Pulling the door shut, she drew her pistol.

Hart gave the order for his men to aim their weapons. When he said "Fire!" the Union army's guns were already blazing. Hart's men had been caught off guard and several crumpled to the ground. They simply were no match for the trained, battle-hardened, Union soldiers. "Shoot! Shoot!" was his command, but the Yankees fired another volley. For the few moments that the moon peeked out and then hid behind the clouds again, the Union soldiers had plenty of time to pick a target. Even in the darkness, their shots hit their marks. Hart's men were so unprepared that they completely missed their shots. Even the dozen Confederate soldiers he was able to bring together missed, as well.

All the front windows were open, each with a rifle pointing out. Even the second-floor bedroom windows were open, and the young black men were being firing downward. All the black women, except Flora, huddled in the kitchen, shielding the younger children. Melton was kneeling down next to his father Jonas, both shooting out of the same parlor window.

The Hart group did manage to do some damage to the outside of the house and some windowpanes were shattered. But their men were falling like ripe peaches from a tree.

"Where are all these bullets comin' from?" Hart cried out.

"I don't know, Papa, but they ain…" a bullet shot him in his gut making him shriek from pain. As he collapsed, his father knelt down next to him.

"Son, are ya hurt?" he touched his son's hand, moving it gently out of the way. When the clouds once again moved from in front of the moon, he saw bright red blood shimmering on his hand. "NO! NO! Son! Don't…don't…" his voice broke as tears streamed out of his eyes.

"Papa…I'm sorry…I was…." That was all he could say, as his young spirit drifted from his now lifeless body.

Benjamin pulled his son back to the carriage. "Help me!" he yelled. One of the Confederate soldiers grabbed James's legs and helped haul him up and into the coach. More shots rang out as the wind blew, and more men dropped in their tracks. "I've gotta get outta here!" Benjamin stuck his neck out of the covered coach and shouted to the driver, "GO!"

"Got anotha' one!" Maggie Mae cried out. She couldn't tell who it was, but she did see a body fall to the ground. The moonshine kept coming and going, so she couldn't tell who was being shot.

"Look, one a dem is leavin'!" Cato shouted.

"Keep shootin'!" Charles ordered. "Shoot until they iz all dead, or they leaves!"

Once the coach had left, the remaining men who were still alive took the hint, mounted their horses and wagons, and followed right behind Hart.

"Looks to me like she's got an army of slaves and they is all sharpshooters, too!" one of the Confederate soldiers exclaimed as he mounted his horse.

"Dey is all leavin' now!" Cato shouted.

"Good! Keep shootin'!"

"No! Stop now! The enemy is in retreat," Sergeant Blackwell ordered.

"Whatever you say, Sergeant." Magnolia Mae got up. "Everyone, stop shootin'! Hold your fire! Chesney, bring some lanterns."

As Chesney brought the lanterns, the rest of the group slowly gathered in the parlor.

A blood-curdling scream came from Lily as she pointed at the lifeless body of her brother, Melton.

Chapter Fifteen

The next morning, Charles, Ned, Willy, and eight of the Yankee soldiers, including Corporal Hughes, went to pick up the dead, to give them a proper Christian burial. They loaded the corpses on the wheelbarrow and, one by one, they took them to the holy field. The rest of the Union soldiers were digging the graves.

"There are a lot of bodies. I never realized we killed so many of them." Corporal Hughes commented.

"Well, Corporal, we picked up twelve bodies."

"'Levun. Das not countin' Melton."

Sergeant Blackwell was saddened by the killing of the young boy. The last thing he wanted was to report to Lieutenant Jenkins was that one of the black children was killed during the attack. He wanted to send him a telegram, but he certainly couldn't go into town. These southerners would never let him send one. Not to mention that the mail was picked up only once a week and by the time he got the news, the boy would be buried for weeks. The only thing he could do was wait.

"Come on, let's hurry along on those graves. These bodies are starting to smell."

The digging went on for two days. Finally, all the dead were buried, and their belongings hidden somewhere inside the house. Maggie Mae did not disclose where she hid them, but she assured Sergeant Blackwell that they were in a secure place.

The Willis family, along with all the women, older girls, and Maggie Mae, were gathered in the parlor praying and mourning the loss of Melton. They didn't want to move him outdoors because the body would begin to decompose quickly. They washed his body, dressed him in Pauly's best Sunday clothes, and laid him on the dining room table. The older girls kept fanning the body to keep the flies away, while the black women adorned him with pretty flowers.

Maggie Mae was devastated. But on the inside, she was fuming. She wanted each and every one of those men to pay for killing a member of her family. *How dare they come in the middle of the night and attack her like that? What right did they have to do that? What rights do I have? Can they really take my plantation away from me? Was that piece of paper real?* So many questions.

"Fanny, we is ready," Charles announced.

Fanny did nothing but nod once. The older boys brought in a casket; freshly made by Cato who had a knack for woodworking and fixing things up around the house. But this, he could not fix. The hatred that those white men had for Negros could not be fixed.

Melton's body was gently moved from the tabletop to the casket, and the cover was nailed on—right after Fanny gave her son one more kiss on the forehead. "You wid' ar' Lord now, Son. Rest in peace," she wailed into her handkerchief.

Willy, Ned, Cato, Jonas, Harry, and Franky picked up the casket and in sync, walked it to the holy field as the rest of the congregation followed behind. They stopped at the deepest grave and laid the casket in evenly, using ropes. As the women wept and threw flowers inside the grave, the men began swiftly covering the boy's casket with dirt.

Charles, being the de facto leader, the patriarch of the group, led the service. "The Lord is my Shepherd; I shall not want. He maketh me to lie down in green pastures. He leadeth me beside the still waters. He restoreth my soul. He leadeth me in the path of righteousness for His name's sake. Yea, though I walk through the valley of the shadow of death, I will fear no evil: for Thou art with me; Thy rod and Thy staff they comfort me. Thou preparest a table before me in the presence of mine enemies: thou anointest my head with oil; my cup runneth over. Surely, goodness and mercy shall follow me all the days of my life: and I will dwell in the house of the LORD forever."

"Dat wuz nice," Fanny managed to say through the tears. She, her family, Maggie Mae, and Sergeant Blackwell were the last to leave.

"Fanny, come to the house, please?"

"No, Missy Maggie, I'm-a gon' go home." Hunched over, she walked away.

"But…"

"Missy Maggie, I do appreciate yo' concern but please, leave her be. She hurtin' heavy, she is. Very heavy."

"Well, all right, Jonas, but you take care of her and…" she gently touched his arm. "…whatever y'all need…anythin'—ya hear?"

Jonas nodded as he caught up with his wife, placing his arm around her shoulders.

Charles shook his head. "Da's sad. So sad." He started walking towards the house.

"Well, I'm gonna let the mournin' take its proper time and then I'm goin' into town." She walked alongside of him.

"What fa?"

"I'm gonna confront the Mayor. I'm gonna warn him there better be no more of these shenanigans, otherwise, there's gonna be mo' dead and they won't be among my family, I assure you of that."

"Uh, Missy Maggie, ain't dat dangerous?"

"Yes, but I'm gonna be armed to the teeth."

"Well, I dunno, Missy Maggie, ya cain't be walkin' 'round with guns in yo' hands."

"Oh, now, dontcha worry yourself, Charles, I got plenty of places to hide my weapons." A subtle smile showed on her face.

~~~~~~

Valdosta came to be in 1860, after the railroad bypassed nearby Troupville, named after Governor George Troup. At that point, Valdosta became the county seat and most Troupville residents moved there. Troupville was abandoned, for the most part. Valdosta took its name from Troup's plantation, Valdosta. Although a long-standing rumor held that the name meant "vale of beauty," Troup had named it after the Valley of Aosta, or Val d'Osta, in Italy. The name Aosta comes from the Roman Emperor Augustus. Occasionally, the Italian "Val d'Osta" spelling was used for the plantation. Valdosta had been established for only a few months before the war broke out. During the war, it became a refuge for all people who were fleeing the areas of Georgia where the war was actively being fought.

Maggie Mae stormed into the Mayor's office. She had not the first worry about getting hurt because she was well-protected by the Union soldiers standing outside, disguised as slaves. It was September and it was still quite hot, but they all wore heavy wool jackets that Rose had sewed for them with hidden internal pockets that tucked pistols and short-barrel rifles discreetly. "Mr. Mayor, I need to speak with you."

The Mayor got up, tipped his hat, and asked: "Mrs. Moon, what can I do for you?" he knew exactly what her visit was about. He had lost a nephew during the altercation and his sister was not pleased with him.

"I am here to give you and all the plantation owners of this town a warnin'!"

"Mrs. Moon, please let me say that I did not agree to what happened on your land, not one bit."

"Mr. Mayor, I will be honest with you. I don't believe you!"

"Mrs. Moon, how…" he stood up.

"I do believe we buried your nephew on my property." She moved in closer to him. "And I am certain that your sister is not very happy with you right now, is she?"

He didn't move a muscle, but his face darkened.

"I also believe—no, I know that Mr. Hart lost his son James. Am I right?"

He sat down without saying a word. Hart was raging mad with her for killing his son. While he was planning it out, both the mayor and the Sheriff told him that he had no business going to her property and attacking her like that, and that he should have expected that she would defend herself. Now that he was mourning his son, they could not tell him the "I told you so;" it was too early.

"Mr. Mayor, I'll have you know that we gave those twelve men a proper Christian burial and…" she gestured one of the men to bring in a wooden crate. "…these are their belongings…" the create was placed on the Mayor's desk. "Each man's possessions are packed inside their own bag. Can I be sure you will distribute these possessions to their rightful owners?"

The Mayor picked up the crate and placed it on the floor next to his desk. "Yes, Mrs. Moon."

"Before I go, I demand that you tell those evildoers to leave me and my plantation be. Do you understand?"

"I do." He knew well that the Terrys were best friends with Sheriff Coulter, and that he had taught her how to shoot as a child.

"Good." She turned to leave.

He was relieved to see her go. He thought she was going to pull out that pistol that he knew she had hidden in her bosom and shoot him. And all for what? Hart and his cronies? No, he would make certain that nobody ever tried something like that again. He didn't want to be held responsible for more dead men—or any of his relatives, for that matter.

Once out the Mayor's office, she made a beeline for the Sheriff's office. Sheriff Coulter was outside, sitting on the bench, puffing on his cigar. When he saw her approaching, he put out his cigar on the heel of his boot and stood up.

"Maggie Mae Terry, how are you?"

She stopped about a foot in front of him and put her hands on her hips. "That's Mrs. Moon."

He tipped his hat. "Well, all right then, Mrs. Moon. To what do I owe the pleasure?"

"Sheriff Coulter, you are aware of the vicious attack that took place on my property?"

"Unfortunately, I am." He frowned. He had known ahead of time that it would turn sour. He knew the Terrys very well. The old man Terry taught his daughter how to shoot and she had been taught to fight for what was right.

"Yes, that was unfortunate but I'm warning you, if this happens again, I will make sure that nobody goes home alive." She pointed her finger at him. "Don't you or them think that I'm helpless or weak or afraid to defend myself, because I am not."

"Well, you proved that the other night, didn't you?"

"I most certainly did, and I will defend MY property with every fiber of my being. Are we clear, Sheriff Coulter?"

"Very." He was angry. Not with Maggie Mae, but with Hart. He warned him that attacking her plantation was a bad idea. People came to Valdosta to escape the war, and Hart's greed got his son killed and brought the war to this quiet town. Well, no more! Not while he was the sheriff.

Suddenly, she smiled warmly at him. "Well, all right, you have yourself a mighty fine day, Sheriff Coulter. And please give my regards to Mrs. Coulter." She turned and started walking towards the general store. "Bring the wagon to the general store boys, I'm gonna buy some staples."

"Mrs. Moon, what brings you here?" Mrs. Potters interrupted stocking the shelves with canned goods.

"I'll handle this. darling. Can you please go to the back?" Mr. Potters looked at his wife the way he does when he wants some privacy with a customer. Besides, she is the one who informed Hart of every move Mrs. Moon made. Well, that was about to end as well. He so happened to be quite fond of Maggie Mae Moon and she was one of his best customers. She always paid top dollar for seeds, just like her father did. His seeds always yielded the best crop and when the Terrys had a good crop, they would always spend their earnings in the Potters' General Store.

"Fine." Mrs. Potters removed her apron, stuck her nose up at Maggie Mae, and left the store.

"Mrs. Moon, I must say that I'm mortified about what happened to you. I trust that y'all are all right."

Maggie Mae saw the sincerity in his eyes. "Thank you, Mr. Potters, I truly appreciate that." She roamed around the store admiring the new fabrics that had just arrived from England. She touched them briefly but then headed directly for the staples.

"What can I get you today?"

"The usual. Flour, sugar, coffee, tea, salt, black pepper, vinegar, and lard. Oh, and some rice."

"The usual amounts?"

"Oh, no I need at least double the usual. I have several new slaves and they need to eat, too, don't they?"

"Yes, indeed. Double it is."

She picked up several kinds of candy and brought it over to Mr. Potters. "and these as well."

He weighed them and placed all the food items in paper bags. "How about some flax seed? I reckon it's time you sell your crop, isn't it?"

"Already done."

"Oh, is that so? I didn't see ya comin' to market with it."

Maggie Mae was caught a bit off guard. She didn't want anyone to know who she sold her crop to. "I didn't. I went to Atlanta this time. I have not been happy with the prices I've been offered after my dear husband passed, bless his soul."

"That is quite a long ride, Mrs. Moon. I hope you got what you wanted for it."

"I did, thank ya Mr. Potters and yes, I'll need some flax while you're at it."

He knew she would not let him down. "Good because I saved my best flax seed just for you, Mrs. Moon." He gave her a big smile.

"Well, you spoil me so." She smiled back. He was probably the most honest man she had ever met. But his wife, oh no, she was a viper of the worst kind.

After her slaves collected all the goods and securely placed them on the wagon, Maggie Mae paid her bill. In full.

"Thank you, Mrs. Moon. It's always a pleasure to do business with you."

"Likewise." She said happily as she headed for the door. "Oh, and Mr. Potters…" she stopped and turned towards him. "And please let Mrs. Potters know that I am sorry for the loss of her nephew." She opened the door and headed out.

"I will." He nodded in discontent. What was that scoundrel thinking? He could never stand his brother in law. He was always a pompous ass acting like he was the king of the world. Well, Benjamin Hart got exactly what was coming to him. He only hoped that with the loss of his son, he would grow in humility. But he had his doubts.

Chapter Sixteen

In early February 1864, Union General Truman A. Seymour began amassing troops in Hilton Head, South Carolina, in preparation to head into Florida. An expeditionary force landed in Jacksonville on February 7, almost two years after the North had originally seized it in March 1862. This was the fourth occupation of Jacksonville by the Union.

The Confederacy had noted the northern troops' movements in South Carolina, and General Beauregard anticipated that the target would be north Florida. Brigadier Generals Joseph Finegan and Alfred Colquitt were tasked with defending Florida against this incursion. General Seymour's men made small incursions into nearby locations, and before long, it became evident that he was preparing to head west, presumably toward Tallahassee, which was contrary to the orders given him. The purpose of Seymour's movement was to disrupt the Confederate food supply from central Florida, disrupt transportation links, capture cotton, turpentine, and timber, recruit blacks for the Union army, and to encourage Unionists in eastern Florida to organize a state government that would be loyal to the United States.

At that point, General Finegan began looking for the best location to thwart Seymour's march. Finegan found this location in Olustee, from the Creek Indian word for "Black Water." Olustee is a strategic position in Florida; south of Jacksonville, a few miles east of Gainesville and set in the middle of the state.

Olustee gave a perfect location at which to meet the Union troops, as there is a narrow passageway between Ocean Lake and a large, swampy area. The Confederate troops could control the battle, that way. Gen. Finegan had put out a call for troops to defend Florida, and Gen. Colquitt brought experienced, battle-hardened troops from Savannah. Gen. Finegan sent small groups of soldiers out to encounter the Union troops and lure them toward Olustee. That move was successful.

On February 20, 1864, 5,500 Union soldiers and 16 cannon headed west from Macclenny. The confederate force was equivalent in size, including the Eighth United States Colored Troops. The Union troops went right where the Confederates wanted them to, which was between Ocean Lake and the swamp. This was a pristine pine forest with very little underbrush. Neither side had constructed any earthworks. The Confederates had formed a line consisting of the infantry in the center, with cavalry flanking them on either side. The ground was quickly becoming dotted by the bodies of the fallen. The colored troops came up to fill the shortages suffered by the Union army.

The Confederates began to run short of ammunition and the Union commanders, including Wesley, noticed them milling around, searching the bodies of their dead comrades—stripping them of weapons, ammunition, water, and anything else they could get their hands on. The Yankees believed that they would have the advantage very soon. But the Rebels managed to get some ammunition from a train car parked just under a mile away. They filled every pocket and pouch with enough ammunition and reinforced their advantage over the Northerners.

Around four in the afternoon, Wesley's orders were to march into battle, after removing all extraneous gear. This reduction in weight allowing them to move much more quickly and quietly, which temporarily eliminated the Rebels' advantage. However, it was only the cover of a strategic withdrawal by the Union forces.

As the evening fell upon the battlefield, the Union retreated in a line and fired behind to the Rebels who had gained considerable ground over them. But as they quickly moved out of harm's way, they heard the Confederate calls to not pursue the Yanks.

As nightfall finally came upon the tired and weary Union soldiers, it was later written:

"Under one of the most terrible fires I ever witnessed, and here on the field of Olustee, was decided whether the colored man had the courage to stand without shelter, and run the dangers of the battlefield, and when I tell you that they stand with a fire in front, on their flank without flinching, I have no doubt as to the center of every man who has gratitude for the defenders of his country, white or black."

That evening, before he went to sleep, Wesley wrote the major events of that day in his notebook:

Our men were dedicated, there is no doubt. Most of them, however, were highly inexperienced in battle. The battle came up quickly and caught most unawares. Many were shot down before they could get their weapons loaded and ready for fire. The rounds and cannonballs came whizzing past. The men watched as their friends were struck and fell bleeding. The sounds of the wounded, screaming in pain, could be heard all around. Many men lost hands, feet, arms, and legs. We were stomping over bodies that already littered the ground. The blood of our brothers in arms was all over us. A man was with us one moment, and in an instant, gone! The odor of spent gunpowder permeated our heads, burning its way in. Many men—actually, young boys, crouched down, trying to avoid the barrage coming their way. Eventually, I was able to get them united into a fighting force, got their senses restored, and got them firing. Many had not fired a weapon before, and so their aim left something to be desired. However, with the sheer number of Confederates, many shots hit a mark, anyway. Colonel Fribley took it upon himself to order a retreat, firing back as we went. Suddenly, shot right through the heart, he fell—lifeless and motionless. That was extremely demoralizing for the men.

At dawn on the 21st, all the survivors were ordered to go around the battlefield and collect the bodies for burial. Wesley wanted to help with the cadaver collections, but he had to report to Col. Fribley's replacement to listen and note the final numbers of the Battle of Olustee: 1861 Union casualties, including 203 dead. The Confederate casualties would number 946, including 93 dead. Wesley had two deaths, 23 wounded, and 3 missing. Since his men were negroes, they likely would receive medical attention only after the white soldiers were taken care of. Hence, he feared, the 23 wounded would join the two who had perished.

"This is by far the worst battle I've ever been in," he remarked.

"Indeed," Was the reply of an unnamed man.

The Battle of Olustee was the largest fought in Florida, and one of the bloodiest of the entire war.

Once all the dead were collected, the numbers were marked in the official documents. The Union soldiers headed back to Jacksonville and stayed there until the war's end.

After Wesley had arrived back in Jacksonville, he went searching for a map. He looked up Valdosta and Jacksonville. He measured about 120 miles.

"That will be a good day's ride," he whispered to himself. He smiled and rolled up the map. He packed a few things in his saddlebags, and prepared for bed. As he had been doing since he arrived in Florida, he pulled out his Bible and read a few passages. Then he took the photograph of his beloved Maggie Mae and kissed it lightly. "Tomorrow, I shall see you again, my love." He slid it to mark the place he left off, closed the Bible, and placed it under his pillow.

Chapter Seventeen

When he arrived at Magnolia Blossom Plantation, he perceived an eerie silence. He wandered over to the barracks where his men were and quietly entered his quarters. He put down his bag and headed outside to greet his soldiers. As soon as Sergeant Blackwell saw him, he raced up and greeted him warmly.

"Lieutenant! So glad to see you!"

"Thank you, Sergeant. It's great to be back."

The rest of the men gathered around the Sergeant and the Lieutenant. But nobody said a word.

"What's going on? Why the glum faces?"

"Well, I suppose you're going to find out sooner or later..."

Wesley's face darkened. "What happened?"

"There was another attack on the plantation, just like last time, except this time there were some killings."

"What? Is Mag... I-I mean Mrs...."

"Yes, she's fine, but one of the negro boys was killed."

He lowered his head. He had failed to follow orders. "I failed him."

Wesley was relieved. But he didn't say a word. He simply patted his sergeant on the back and nodded. Then he asked: "I know you did the best you could. Who was it?"

"Melton."

"Oh, how tragic." He had taught the boy to shoot and he was a quick learner.

"Indeed…but we killed eleven of them."

Wesley was impressed.

"Do you know who they were?"

"Yes. Mrs. Moon had them buried right over there…" he pointed to the fresh gravesites that were being overtaken by weeds. "She collected all their belongings and took them to the mayor."

"She did?"

"Yes, I went with her."

"Good. I'm glad she didn't go alone."

"Oh yes. I was not going to let anything happen to her."

"What did the mayor have to say?"

"I don't know. I didn't go in, but I did notice the beat-up look on his face."

"Ah, I see." Wesley grinned as he imagined her giving the mayor her what-for.

"Oh, and here's the best part. That Mr. Hart who is the head of the pack, his son perished during the attack. A shot fired by Melton, himself!"

Wesley was silent for a moment, taking it all in. "When did all this happen?"

"Last August."

"Last August? And nobody wrote me about it?" he was irritated that all this time passed.

"We tried Lieutenant, but we couldn't get ahold of you."

Wesley realized that Sergeant Blackwell was right. The mail was extremely slow, and telegrams were difficult to send—especially during the battles. "I suppose you're right. Didn't get much of anything during the battle of Olustee."

"Olustee? Where's that?"

"In Florida, about seventy-five miles southeast from here."

"Did we win?"

Wesley shook his head. "Nah. Not this one."

"Too bad."

"Yes. On that note; everyone to your barracks. Get some rest. Tomorrow we'll meet and talk about what's next."

The men began to return to their quarters, mumbling their goodnights as they disappeared.

Instead of going to bed, Wesley decided to take a walk to the main house. He hoped his beloved was up. But as he approached, her light was off and the window was closed.

"That's all right. Rest my love. I shall see you tomorrow," he whispered.

~~~~~~

The sound of children laughing awakened the lieutenant. Right off the bat, he recognized Pauly, Jupiter, Lewis, Joseph, Will, Henry, Roby, and Peter. It sounded as though they were playing war. He got up, slipped on his trousers, and opened the door. The boys recognized him immediately. They cried for joy and huddled around him.

"Lieutenant Jenkins!" Pauly shouted.

"Lieutenant Jenkins, when you get back?" Henry asked.

"Late last night." He shook all the young men's hands. "Shouldn't you boys be working in the fields today?"

"Nah, itz Sundee." Roby proudly stated.

"Ah, I see." He ruffled Pauly's silky, reddish-blonde hair. "Did Charles have his service yet?"

Sunday was Charles's day. He collected everyone in the back of the house and preached the Gospel. Since black folk were not allowed to attend Sunday services in town, he led them, and from what Maggie Mae had told Wesley, he's been doing it for years now.

"Not yet, but he'll be ringin' his bell soon."

"All right, well you best be getting ready then. Go on!" Wesley commanded the boys and they all tore away heading for their houses.

As Wesley approached the house, the scent of Chesney's southern cooking wafted through the air. It was something he missed very dearly while in Florida—more so than his grandmother's cooking. He only hoped his grandmother was not rolling in her grave. He opened the door and peeked in. "What's for breakfast?"

Chesney almost dropped the pot of grits she was stirring. "Wesley! You dun scar't the wits outta me!" She cleaned her hands on her apron and gave Wesley a warm hug.

He swept Chesney off her feet and twirled her around. "I'm so glad to be back and…" he gently put her down and kissed her cheek. He had become fond of this new family, and especially of Chesney because she had cooked her way to his heart. "...I'm hungry." He sat down at the large, massive oak table.

"Ah, boy! You were missed 'round 'ere." She stirred the grits again. Then she took a plate, plopped some scrambled eggs, sausage, bacon, and home fries on it, and placed it in front of him.

"Mmmmm...Chesney...this looks heavenly."

Then a small bowl of grits suddenly appeared in front of him with a bit of butter melting in the middle of it.

"Grits? Ah, no, I can't have these." He just had not been able to acquire the taste.

"Now, boy, ya needs ta eat dem grits cuz all dis don't taste right wit'out 'em. Now, go on." She shoved the small bowl right under his face.

He looked at her and smiled. "Fine," and began pecking at them.

"Yessum. Dat'z right. Brekfus' jus' ain't brekfus' without dem grits."

As he was chowing down his much-desired breakfast, he heard a familiar voice coming from the hallway.

"…Now, you best not be lyin' to…" Maggie Mae froze when she saw Wesley enjoying his breakfast. "Wesley!" her eyes lit up.

He gulped down his last bite.

"See, Mama? I dun told ya I'd seen him." Pauly quickly went and sat next to the Union soldier.

"Yes, I s'pose you were right." She sat right across from her beloved. "Are you all right?" she wanted to kiss him, but she had to contain herself.

"Yes, I'm fine."

"Ain't dat sum su'prize, Missy Maggie?" she was beaming with delight.

"Yes, Chesney, some surprise, indeed." Maggie Mae found it nigh impossible to take her eyes off him. "When did you get back?" She gently rubbed on the brooch he had left her.

"Late last night." He could not take his eyes off her and off the brooch that sparkled like her blue sapphire eyes. He had ached so much after he left.

"Where from?"

"Florida. Jacksonville, to be precise."

"I know where it is. I went there once with Daddy when I was a girl. Lively town."

"Not very lively now with this war going on." He finished gulping down his food. He even finished the grits so he wouldn't have to hear Chesney again.

"I can imagine."

He noticed she was looking fabulous in her plaid blue and black dress with matching jacket. It was still quite brisk outside. "You look splendid." He got up and moved closer to her.

"Thank you." She moved closer to him.

He opened his arms and she embraced him. She closed her eyes to take in his essence, his strength, his gentleness, and his love.

Chesney whispered something in Pauly's ear and led him out of the kitchen, leaving them completely alone. He smiled and waved as he left.

Wesley caressed her obsidian curly hair and gently rubbed her neck. Her perfume of sweet Georgia peaches and freshly whipped cream was unbearable, but he maintained his military composure. "You have no idea how much I've missed you."

She slid her right hand down his face. She could feel the cheerlessness on his face and in his heart. "I feel your heavy heart."

He took her hand and kissed it on her palm. "This war…" he placed it over his heart. "it places man against man, town against town, city against city, and there are no winners, only brokenness and demise."

"Darling, what horrible things you must have seen."

"Undoubtedly. I genuinely pray that this gruesome war will end soon.

"So do I, my darling, so do I."

He sat her down. "I was sorry to hear about Melton."

"Oh, it was devastating! Fanny and Jonas are besides themselves. I cannot fathom burying a child; I simply cannot."

"It's not right." He sat in the chair next to her. "Has anyone bothered you since?"

"Oh no. I made it perfectly clear to both the mayor and the sheriff that I will not tolerate another attack like that. I will surely defend this land until my dying day."

"I'll be here, by your side."

"Oh, darling, I am so grateful you didn't take all your men with you, 'cause if you did, I honestly don't know if we'd all be alive today."

"Not to worry. I would not have left you without protection. I knew well that those vile men would attempt to take your land. Besides, we had plenty of Union soldiers in Olustee, but we lost just the same."

"You did?" she frowned. "Those damned Rebels!"

"You needn't worry yourself. I'm not going anywhere for a while."

Maggie Mae gave him a sexy look, took his hand, and led him upstairs—just as Charles entered the kitchen. They didn't even notice he was there, and he didn't say a word. He watched them go up the stairs together. He sighed and shook his head. *'Dis ain't gon' end well, it ain't.*

~~~~~~

Over the summer, Wesley and Maggie Mae became inseparable, and despite what Harriet and Charles warned them about the consequences of their actions, they ignored them. They would go on picnics. They would go horseback riding. They would all eat together under the back porch every evening and tell stories to the children when the moon and the stars came out.

The children became fond of one story, in particular: Joseph and his Puppies

There once was a boy named Joseph who found four puppies; three of them had soft, smooth, chocolate brown fur and were perfect. The fourth one had rough, spotty, light and dark brown fur and wasn't as perfect.

Joseph loved all four of the but tended to play more with the fourth one. One morning, Joseph went to feed the puppies and found only the three perfect ones. He searched the yard for the fourth and called him. Then he noticed the open gate.

"Oh, my, Spotty must have run off."

Two days passed. Joseph still had the three perfect puppies, but he missed his Spotty terribly. The next night, he heard yapping, and when he saw it was Spotty, Joseph was thrilled. The puppy had been lost and now was found. After that day, Joseph made sure that his puppies would never be separated, ever again.

"Dis is jus' like Luke 15:7—there is more rejoicing in heaven over one found soul than for ninety-nine souls who were never lost," Charles recited. He always took the opportunity to teach all the children, young and old, about the Word of God.

Right after the fourth of July, Maggie Mae caught word that some of the Union soldiers would be leaving, and it was rumored that Wesley was going to lead them again.

When he went to the parlor that evening to have his usual conversation with his beloved while sipping evening tea, he found Maggie Mae unsettled and pacing around.

"My darling, what is troubling you?"

"I heard you're leavin' again. Did I hear right?"

"I-we…"

"You promised you were gonna stay, an' now you're leavin'. Again! This is unfair! Unfair!" She turned her back to him as tears streamed down her face.

He clutched her shoulders and pulled her to his chest. "Maggie, I promise you, I'm not leaving."

Wiping her nose with her handkerchief. "You're not?"

"No."

"But I heard…"

"I'm sending Sergeant Blackwell, with another group of men. The men that were with me, will be staying here…" he turned her around. "…with me."

"Oh, darling!" she was so happy she jumped up to kiss him, as he stood a good foot taller than she.

Harriet was eavesdropping from the hallway, disappointed that Wesley was not leaving. She thought he needed to leave, because her mistress was falling for him again. She shook her head and whispered to herself: "Dis ain't gud, ain't no gud, no how."

Chapter Eighteen

When the cotton was ready for picking this time, Maggie Mae decided to sell it to the Northerner again. She was confident that he would pay her very well for this magnificent crop. He did not disappoint. He went to visit the plantation late one September evening, paid her well, and complimented her for the extraordinary quality of the cotton.

"How do you do it, Mrs. Moon?" he was a gaunt, middle-aged, rather short man, bald with a handlebar moustache. "Your crops are magnificent!"

"Well, it's quite simple, really. You attract more flies with honey than with vinegar. That's what my Daddy used to say."

"You see, Mr. Banner, it seems that Mr. Terry always treated his slaves like they were family, and in turn, they worked voluntarily for him. He never beat them, nor did he treat them like animals. No, he treated them with dignity and respect, and they loved him like a father."

"That's correct. And now that Daddy has passed, God rest his soul, Charles Willis is the patriarch of Magnolia Blossom Plantation." She proudly said.

"Well, it works because I have never seen such quality cotton such as this." He reached into the bales and took out a handful of the white gold. "Excellent!" He shoved the sample into his jacket pocket. Then he pulled out a large, black leather portfolio, opened it and pulled out some Union dollars.

"Do you have any Confederate money?" Maggie Mae asked since she couldn't buy staples with Union money.

Mr. Banner reached inside his front jacket pocket and pulled out a roll of Confederate bills. "How much do you need, Mrs. Moon?"

"Well, how much are you paying me per pound?"

He looked at Wesley and smiled. "I can offer you $1.45 per pound. Do we have a deal?"

Maggie Mae's heart raced. Nobody had ever offered her that much for her cotton, never. She extended her gloved hand to Mr. Banner. "Yes."

"Well, all right." He called over to a few of Wesley's men. "You three, over there."

"Yes, sir." They all headed towards him.

"Please, can you weigh these here bales?"

They nodded and began pulling the bales out passing them to each other, bucket brigade style. Each bale was weighed, and the weight shouted to Mr. Banner. He noted the weight in his little notebook. Then he tallied up the weight. "Mrs. Moon, I note a total of 997 pounds."

Maggie Mae was astounded and could not muster words. She nodded.

"Very well. How about I give you one hundred Confederate dollars and the rest in Union dollars? Will that work for you Mrs. Moon?"

"Yes, Mr. Banner, that's fine." This would give her enough to pay the workers and have plenty to buy staples. "Please come inside. It's cooler in there."

Mr. Banner followed Maggie Mae into the dining room and began counting the money, placing it in piles on the oak dining room table. Once he completed his task, he gathered his things, but Maggie Mae stopped him.

"Mr. Banner, would you do us the honor of joinin' us fa supper?"

"Mrs. Moon, believe me, from those aromas coming out of that kitchen, I would love to stay, but it's too risky."

"Come now, Mr. Banner, there's nobody around here that will hurt you. It is just us. Besides, if anybody dares to set foot on this land, they will be met with guns a-blazing," Wesley assured him.

Mr. Banner scratched his head and smiled. "Very well, I shall accept your invitation."

"Oh, good. Fanny, please add a place for our guest, if you would."

"Yes'm, right away." Fanny went to the heavy, walnut buffet, and pulled out a tablecloth, some napkins, plates, silverware, and crystal goblets. She quickly set up the dining room table while Maggie Mae, Wesley, and Mr. Banner headed toward the parlor.

After twenty minutes or so, Fanny called out, "Come an' git it!" At that, the group made their way into the dining room. Pauly and Lizzie ran down the stairs, nearly tripping over each other. Fanny brought out platter after platter of delectable, typical southern Georgia cuisine, like Pork Roast and White Beans, Pot Roast, Sweet and Spicy Chicken, Corn on the Cob, Mashed Potatoes, White Gravy, Green Bean Casserole, Peach Cobbler, Apple Pie, and Prune Cake with plenty of wine to brighten the mood.

"My goodness, Mrs. Moon. I have never eaten so much in my entire life!" Mr. Banner rubbed his belly. "Truly delicious, indeed!"

"Why, thank ya, Mr. Banner."

After dinner, everyone went to the back porch to enjoy a cigar, some brandy, and small talk. Instead of the sounds of rifles and cannons, music filled the air. The fiddle, banjo, and guitar came out and the evening air was filled with singing, dancing, and cheerfulness. The younger children began to dance right away, and then the adults joined in. In the end, even Charles and Harriet danced. Everyone had a grand old time, and by the time Mr. Banner was escorted to his coach by several of Wesley's men, it was one in the morning.

Before Maggie Mae headed up to her room, she put all the money away in her secret hiding place while Wesley kept a vigil eye.

"I still can't believe how much Mr. Banner paid for my cotton!"

"I told you. I knew he was going to pay you more than those crooks at the market."

"Yes, you were right." She covered the floor with the rug and headed for the stairs. "Are ya comin'?" She reached for his hand.

Wesley gave her a sensual look and took her hand. "Of course, darling."

Charles was entering the kitchen and was heading for the guest room where he had been sleeping since Maggie Mae had been widowed. He heard the whispering and giggling of the newly reunited couple and shook his head. He did not like how they were carrying on and he was going to have a talk with the Union Lieutenant soon.

Embraced by the warmth of the lively fire that was warming her room, Maggie Mae undid the buttons of her blouse and tossed it off her shoulders. In a ballet of naive exhibitionism, she arched her back and lowered her arms to allow the blouse to fall from her porcelain shoulders. She tossed the blouse aside and said, "Wesley, are you gaping."

"I'm not gaping. Smirking, maybe. Grinning, possibly. But gaping? Definitely not gaping. And if I am gaping, I deserve to be gaping, even though I'm not." Wesley, who was most definitely gaping, was thinking that this woman was a gift from God. He found it impossible to turn his head from Maggie Mae's breasts; they seemed to defy gravity as they floated. Soon, he forced his eyes from her rosy crests and found that she was looking directly at him.

"Wesley, are you going to just stand there all night?"

After realizing that he was obviously gaping, and on the verge of drooling, he said, "yes…uh…no…"

"I'll see what I can do to help," she said, and moved closer. When they were only inches apart, he slid his hands up her slender waist and surrounded both breasts, slowly rubbing her nipples with the pads of his thumbs. His hands squeezed and rotated.

Maggie Mae purred, "Oh, Wesley," and arched into his body. "I've missed you so much, I've ached." Their lips moved closer and touched. His tongue reached out and her lips opened to allow it entry. Her hands moved around his neck and she stroked her fingers through his curly hair. As their tongues danced and his hands caressed her, they both leaned slightly, lost their balance, and fell against the lamp table.

Laughing, they regained their balance and returned to a half-seated position. Their eyes gradually met. Wesley lowered his head and began nibbling and kissing as he progressed down her neck. He continued his downward excursion until his lips locked onto a quivering nipple, his tongue charting the perimeter of the swollen tip. His hand stroked its twin. Both rosy peaks were throbbing; one in his hand, the other between his lips.

Maggie Mae sighed, and as she shook her head, tossing her obsidian curls back, "The bed...the bed..." was all that she could say between her labored breaths.

He flipped the covers on the bed, picked her up, and gently placed her on it.

Breathlessly, "Wesley…" came from her, as she ran her palms from his hard, lean stomach around to his back and slowly pulled him closer.

He could feel her nipples as they pushed and strained against his skin as though they were trying to siphon nourishment from him.

He answered, "What, my darling?" and moved his hand to the downy curls between her legs and slipped his finger partially into her wetness.

With a quick and shallow breath, she parted her legs slightly. "Ahhhh…" she groaned.

He leaned over, kissed her, and synchronized the rhythms of his tongue and finger.

"This…is. I've never…" she said, gasping at the ever-deepening strokes probing into her slippery softness.

Wesley looked a little surprised and said, "You've never…what?" he said and added a mate to the finger still inside Maggie Mae.

"…never felt anything like this…ever…ahhh…" Maggie Mae felt herself tighten around the fingers that soon would be replaced with something even better.

As he maneuvered to remove his trousers, her hands slowly encircled his waist and gently nudged him closer. Their lips touched, her breasts were against his, her rose-tipped nipples again burrowing into his flesh.

His pulsating manhood was strategically positioned between her legs, and Maggie Mae slowly parted them so that the throbbing head of his erection could slowly pass along the sensitive valley of her womanly desires. She gently thrust her hips upward and found that by doing so, his hot flesh nestled in the warm, moist folds of the portal to her femininity. She continued in this sensual rhythm as her breathing became deeper and unsteady.

"Oh, Wesley! This…feels…so…GOOD!" She managed to push these words out between thrusts as her hands massaged the rippling planes of his muscular back in a motion that matched the rhythmic pulsations that each had developed. Between labored breaths and frenzied writhing, she continued, "my Lord!"

Wesley settled his entire weight on her writhing body. As they kissed, he guided himself into her passion-moistened depths, and slowly, carefully eased himself just barely inside her.

Maggie Mae clenched and shuddered and raised her hips slightly to further drive his swollen saber into her hot, wet sheath. Wesley lowered himself again and, as Maggie Mae heaved in passion, her resisting flesh split, and he slid into her slowly and gently until he was completely inside her.

"Are you all right?" he asked when, suddenly, she encircled him with her legs and forced him even deeper. He could feel her pulsating -- contracting and releasing his erection until he eased himself back for fear that he would explode.

"I'm very fine," was the verbal reply, but her body language said much more as they began bucking and arching and colliding in almost perfect rhythm. With every withdrawal, she arched her hips and heaved beneath him, so as to protest the removal of something that she now claimed as her own, if only for the moment. "Oh…oh…oh…!" came in ever louder and higher pitched moans.

Wesley kept up the rhythm that Maggie Mae had set and maintained it relentlessly. With each stroke, he slid his engorged flesh completely into her hot, humid depths. Their breathing came in gasps—as though the air had thinned. His mouth pressed against her neck. His breathing was fast and furious. Maggie Mae's breaths came in punctuated gasps.

He could no longer resist the increasing passion, her wriggling against him, her sighs, her legs pulling him into her ever deeper. With one final thrust, he shuddered and exploded inside her.

She could feel his seed spill into her moist depths. Dazed and motionless, but still deep inside Maggie Mae, Wesley could feel her early spasms contracting against his manhood. He began a slow, short, rhythmic stroking that soon became full length plunges of his still-aroused flesh. Maggie Mae began to heave and writhe, naked flesh against naked flesh. Wesley increased the pace and deepened the penetration. Each thrust brought a corresponding reply, when suddenly Maggie Mae reached around Wesley, pulled him against her, and began gyrating and grinding herself into him. "Yes…yes…oh…oh…" she heaved and convulsed into a chain of explosions. She screamed, as the sensual waves continued as Maggie Mae was seized by great shuddering clenching spasms that squeezed and milked the throbbing heat within.

The next morning, the aroma of Chesney's breakfast seeped up to Maggie Mae's bedroom. Wesley's stomach woke him up first. He gently tapped her slumbering body.

"Mmmmm…" she groaned and turned over.

He smiled and shrugged his shoulders. "I'm going down for some breakfast," He whispered in her ear.

She didn't budge. So, he dressed quickly and made his way down to the kitchen.

Chesney was stirring the grits again as he entered the room and sat down.

"Mornin' Chesney! How are you today?"

She turned and gave him a sly smile. "Well, I see yo is havin' a mighty fine day." She set up a plate and placed it in front of him.

"I sure am." He began gobbling down his breakfast.

Charles walked in and gave Wesley a stern look. Wesley stopped eating. He already knew what he was going to be scolded about.

Chapter Nineteen

"A wedding? How exciting! Who's gettin' married?"

"Molley."

"Molley?" Maggie Mae gave Rose a warm hug. "I'm so happy for ya, Rose!" she was tickled that there was going to be a wedding on her plantation. "So, tell me, who's the groom?"

"One of dem Yankees, Isaac Hughes. He a Corp'ral."

"I see. So, she'll be goin' up north then?"

"Yessum, right afta' dis war ends." Her face turned dour.

"Oh, don't worry. She will be all right. You'll see." She patted Rose's hand.

"I gots a request."

"What is it?"

"I gots ta sew her a dress and I was thinkin'…"

"Oh, don't say another word." She took her hand and led her upstairs. Rose almost stumbled as she climbed the stairs. They giggled. "Here we are." They entered Maggie's parents' bedroom which had been kept as it was when her father passed. She opened up her mother's armoire. "Here you go."

Rose hesitated. "Are ya sure, Missy Maggie?"

"Absolutely! Molley deserves a pretty dress." She stepped back to allow Rose to sip through the dresses.

Rose pulled out a few of them but when she noticed a light pink, silk brocade one with matching jacket and hat, she pulled it out. "Oh, yes, I rememba dis one." Her eyes brightened. "It looked perfect on yo' mama."

"It sure did." She pulled it out and placed it in Rose's arms. "It's yours. No. Molley's now."

Rose hugged it to her breast. "Tank ya Missy Maggie, tank ya!"

"Ah, don't mention it! Now, go on, go create your masterpiece." The joy in Rose's eyes warmed her heart.

~~~~~~

On October 1, 1864, the plantation was all decked out for a joyous wedding between Molley Steward and Corporal Isaac Hughes. The back garden was all set up with all the chairs that the plantation had made available to use, along with several benches prepared in haste by the Union soldiers. Cato had made an arch from wood and the younger girls dressed it up with wildflowers and pieces of ribbon that Rose had found.

All the Union soldiers, including Wesley, were dressed in their freshly-cleaned uniforms, all standing behind Corporal Hughes waiting for the bride to appear.

Seated in the front row seats were Rose, Lana, Henry Matilda, Betsy, and Will—along with Maggie Mae and Harriet, all dressed in their finest outfits.

Maggie Mae was magnificent in her fuchsia gown. It was the first time that Wesley had seen her in it. Her raging curls were pulled up and held by pins and small combs with just a smidge of color on her lips. She covered her bare shoulders with a black shawl crocheted for her by her paternal grandmother, Elizabeth, after whom she had named her daughter. Wesley could not take his eyes off her, and had a growing desire that wouldn't placate.

The rest of the family were seated in the remaining chairs and benches. There weren't enough to accommodate everyone, so all the older children and men stood patiently behind the seats.

When the bride and her father Ned showed up at the kitchen door, the few soldiers who played instruments began the wedding march and everyone stood up.

As Ned proudly began walking his eighteen-year-old daughter down the aisle, his smile glistened as his tears shone in the bright Georgia sunlight.

"Oh, my, Rose! That dress is a true masterwork. How did you do that?" Maggie whispered in Rose's ear.

Rose shrugged and smiled. She was enormously proud of what she had created from an old garment. Her heart filled with joy as she caught her daughter's attention.

"Love you, Mama," her daughter silently worded.

"Love you, too." Rose silently responded as she waved at her handsome husband.

Charles was waiting for them, standing on a platform that the male slaves had built for the occasion. "Who gives away this beautiful bride?"

"I do." Ned kissed his daughter on the cheek and handed her over to Isaac. "Ya better take care of her, ya heah?"

"Yes, sir, I promise." Isaac hooked his bride's arm into his and faced Charles.

"We are gathered here today to join these two young'ns in holy matrimony. Before I begin, if anyone has any reason to contest this marriage, speak now or forever hold your peace."

There was no sound except the cardinals and blue jays chirping and singing.

"Very well." He opened his Bible. "Will you please face each other and hold hands."

The couple happily did as instructed.

"Corporal Isaac Hughes, do you take dis woman to be your wedded wife? Will you love her, comfort her, through good times and bad, in sickness and in health, honor her and be faithful to her for as long as you both shall live?"

"I do." Isaac responded with beaming eyes that show his true love for his beloved.

"Molley Ann Steward, do you take dis man to be your wedded husband? Will you love him, comfort him, through good times and bad, in sickness and in health, honor him and be faithful to him for as long as you both shall live?"

"I-I do." She answered with a lump in her throat.

Charles looked to Wesley. "Do ya gots da rings?"

Wesley pulled out two wedding bands. Maggie Mae had donated her parents' wedding bands to the young couple. She had no use for them, and she certainly couldn't go into town to buy any as it would have raised several eyebrows and she didn't want anyone snooping around ruining Molley's special day.

Charles gave the rings to the bride and groom. Then he turned towards the groom and said: "Isaac, please place da ring on Molley's finger and repeat after me: I, Isaac, take you, Molley, to be my wife, to love and cheris' you from dis day forward, and thereto pledge you my faith. Wi' dis ring I thee wed."

Isaac repeated the words precisely.

Then Charles turned to Molley. "Molley, please place da ring on Isaac's finger and repeat after me: I, Molley, take you Isaac to be my husband, to love and cheris' you from this day forward, and thereto pledge you my faith. Wi' dis ring I thee wed."

Molley repeated the words as Charles had spoken them.

"Isaac and Molley, as you have consented together in the union of matrimony and have pledged your faith to each othuh in the presence of this company, now by the authority vested in me, I now pronounce you Husband and Wife. You may kiss the bride, son."

As the newlyweds kissed with abandon, the crowd cheered and clapped loudly and gleefully. The couple turned around to face one of Chesney's brooms lying on the ground and waiting to be jumped over. The crowd began counting-one-two-three and the couple jumped over the broom together. Once again, the crowd cheered and shouted, "Hooray for Isaac and Molley!"

Janette had never seen this done and was curious. "Mama, why did they jump over the broom?"

"Well, we is not allowed ta marry in da courts so we do dis to make our marriages legal in de eyes of our Lord."

"Ah, I see mama. So, did you and daddy do dis too?"

"Yes'm. Se'nteen years ago."

Chesney had prepared an abundant meal for everyone to enjoy. It took her three days to put it together, but when she watched everyone eating with zeal and complimenting her on her cooking, she beamed with pride and joy.

After everyone had filled their tummies, the few musicians began playing lively music.

Everyone was merrily dancing, singing, and having a good time.

Maggie Mae also was having a wonderful time. She was swaying and gliding to the music while being held firmly by her beloved. While she was twirling to a song that must have lasted more than five minutes, she became dizzy and fainted in Wesley's arms. The dancing came to a screeching halt and the music stopped. Wesley laid her gently on the wooden floor just recently built to accommodate the jubilant festivities.

"Air, let her have some air, please." Wesley shouted as he fanned her with his handkerchief. With a frantic look in his eyes, he called to Flora. "Help me please? She's not waking up."

Flora was by his side in an instant and knelt next to her friend.

"Take her upstairs," Harriet commanded.

Charles addressed the wedding party. "Y'all continue wid dis 'ere party; everytin' is gon' be fine,"

"Yes, Mammy." Wesley picked up Maggie and carried her up the stairs and to her room. He was shaking. *What could it be?* He thought but he was afraid of the answer. He just wanted her to wake up. "Wake up Maggie! Wake up!" He laid her on the bed.

The two women began to undress her as Charles walked into the room. Harriet gave him a look to remove Wesley from the room.

"Come on boy, ya gots ta go." He pulled Wesley's sleeve.

"No! I'm not budging. I need her to wake up."

"Boy, ya need ta let da women do their t'ing. Come on, yo can see her later on." He tugged harder this time. "She gon' be fine."

Wesley took one last look at her and followed Charles out.

"She gon' be fine. Ya needn't worry." He patted the young Lieutenant on the back. "Them two is gon' take gud care of her, yo' gon' see."

Wesley was not in the mood to celebrate. He was worried out of his mind that he had done something to hurt his sweetheart. He couldn't lose her! He would rather die in battle than lose her. As he paced up and down the parlor floor, he prayed silently.

Charles wasn't pacing. He stood in the archway, watching Wesley lose his mind. He shook his head and waited patiently for the women to come down with the news. About ten minutes later, both women came down the stairs and entered the parlor. Flora had a semi-happy look on her face, whereas Harriet did not.

"Mammy, what happened? Is she all right?"

"She fine."

"She wants to see ya," Flora said.

Wesley didn't need to be told twice. He ran up the stairs two by two, and was by her side in no time flat.

"Darling." Maggie Mae said as she took Wesley's left hand.

"How are you? Did I do something while we were dancing? I'm so sorry I hurt you."

"Oh, no, no, I'm fine." She placed his hand on her lower tummy. "We are fine." She smiled.

Wesley was puzzled. *What did she mean? We are fine.* He looked into her loving eyes and then it dawned on him. "We?"

She nodded.

"As in you and a baby?" his heart stopped. A child!

She smiled warmly and continued nodding. His deep brown eyes swam with tears as he gazed upon her blue eyes that smiled warmly. "Yes." She said softly.

He had never seen something so wonderful as the soft smile that played upon her lips.

Chapter Twenty

Maggie Mae stayed in bed for a few days. She had asked Wesley and everyone else to stay away. Only Flora was allowed to visit and take care of her. She didn't want to lose this child like she did the last one. She wanted to have Wesley's child even as she feared the townsfolk. A shiver went down her spine just at the thought of what might happen to her if any one of those people found out about her baby. Not only that, they would lynch her, take her plantation, they would kill or sell off all her slaves, and send her children to an orphanage. She rubbed her tummy. "I'm not gonna let that happen, my child, ya hear? Your Mama will protect you." But she was worried, deeply worried. What about Wesley? He can't take care of a child while he's fighting this war! Who knows how long it will last? She was full of questions and anguish.

Wesley was going berserk. After he stayed with his beloved for a few hours, he was asked to leave her be for a few days. Why did he agree to that? Now, he was going crazy and he had to keep his promise. He couldn't go against her will. Besides, Charles, Harriet, and Flora made absolutely sure that he would not pay her a visit. Not to mention that neither Charles nor Harriet had said one word to him since Molley's wedding. That bothered him, too. "Why? What did I do to them?" he asked Chesney one morning.

"Ya want da truth?"

"Yes, of course."

"Dey is mad at ya fo' puttin' Missy Maggie in danger."

"Danger? Why would she be in danger?"

"Why you is as stubborn as a Georgia mule!"

"Why do you say that?"

"I dunno. Alls I know iz dat you puttin' her in danger, is all. Ya gots ta ask papee 'bout dat."

"All right, I will," he said, as he went looking for Charles. He found him at the front of the house, pulling weeds. "Charles, a word please?"

Dressed in his grubby clothes, Charles slowly got up and removed his gloves. "Wut you want, boy?"

"Please, can we talk?"

Charles went to the porch, removed his straw hat, wiped the sweat off his brow, and sat down on the rocker. "Ches! Can we git sum sweet tea?"

"Yessir," was her faint reply from the kitchen.

"Now, wut 'chu wanna talk 'bout, boy?"

"Tell me why I'm being told that I'm putting Maggie Mae in danger. I love her too much. I would never do that."

"Oh, but ya are, son, ya are."

"How so?"

"I dun told ya dis before, don'tcha remember?"

He did. "Yes, but who's going to find out? It's just us here."

Chesney opened the screen door with her foot, laid out the pitcher of sweet tea on the wicker table, poured the tea out for the two men, and went back inside, all without uttering a word.

"Awright den, 'splain dis ta me; what is gon' happen when we needs staples an' such? And wutz gon' happen when she's gotz ta sell her crop?"

"Well, you and I can go into town for staples and Mr. Banner can buy the crops."

"Well, ya see, das not gon' work."

"Why not?"

"We negros ain't allowed to go into town by ourselves to buy t'ings. Dem white folk ain't gonna sell us nuttin'."

"Really?"

"Yessir. Only Missy Maggie can go ta town and buy stuff."

Wesley thought about it for a moment. "Well, how about she writes a letter giving us permission to buy necessities on her behalf?"

Charles burst out laughing. "Nah, dat ain't gon' work. Dey ain't gon' go wid dat."

"Why?"

"Cuz, dey gonna ax, where she be and why she didn't come wid us."

"Ah…but…"

"Ain't no but son, dey is gon' demand ta see her and if dey see her in dem condition, well, dey is gon' lynch her right den and dere, without hesitation."

"No, they wouldn't dare."

"Boy, ya ain't gittin' it. So, I iz gon' tell ya'a story." He took a sip of his tea. "Ah, dat's sum godly nectarine rite dere, it is."

"Yes, I agree. Please continue." Wesley also took a gulp of his tea.

"One time, when I was 'bout 'cho age, a negro dat I knew well dared ta look at a white girl while she was walkin' wid her mama one day and dey caught 'im starin'."

"And?"

"Why dey picked up sum switches and started beatin' up on him, real fierce-like."

"For a look?"

"Yessir. Den later on dat night, dey pulled him outta bed an' lynched him in front his mama." He shook his head as his face turned grim. "Dat boy was my baby brudder, he was." He closed his eyes and looked down at the bed of flowers he'd just planted.

"I'm so sorry."

"Was a long time ago."

"Charles, do you honestly think they would do that horrible thing to Maggie Mae?"

"Yessir, I do. They bin wantin' her land for a while now and dis would be a perfect way to take it."

"I shudder to think something like that could happen to Maggie Mae."

"Same 'ere. I was dere when she wuz born an' now dat both her parents dun gone ta our Lord, I been summon'd wit da task o' bein' her daddy, an' I cain't have anyting happenin' to her, ya understand boy?"

Even the thought of something of what Charles had described frightened him. Even if he took her up north, which was quite dangerous in itself, they still would not be able to live happily due to their diversity. Just because negros were free, didn't mean they were free to marry white women. He was in a predicament and the outcome was utterly hopeless.

"And another ting…if dat child is yours, ya cain't let it grow up wid'out knowin' who da fodder is. Dat ain't right."

"I see your point." He had an idea of how to solve that dilemma.

"What point?" Maggie Mae appeared in the doorway.

"Missy Maggie, how ya feelin'?" Charles got up and motioned her to sit.

"No, that's all right." She looked at Wesley, who was still in awe of her sneaking up on him. "What were you two discussin'?"

"The future."

"Ah, yes, of course. The future."

"How are you feeling?"

"I'm perfectly fine, darlin'." She placed her warm hand on his shoulder and smiled. "Charles, can ya please gather everyone? I need to speak to all y'all."

"Yes'm. I suppose we is ta gather in the back?"

"Yes." Was all she said.

Charles left them alone.

"So, what are you going to say to them?"

"Well, first I need to let them know of my condition."

He moved closer and placed his right hand on her tummy. "How you feelin'?"

"Oh, I'm fine. No need to worry, darlin'."

"I'm so relieved. I honestly thought you were angry with me. Are you?"

"Absolutely not. I just needed a few days to myself to ponder on things, is all."

"I see." He decided he was going to speak to the group right after she was done.

Flora peeked out the front door. "We iz all ready, Missy Maggie."

"Well, all right."

They all made their way to the back of the house. Charles had taken one of the wing chairs from the parlor out onto the back porch so she could sit while she spoke. He figured she was still too weak to stand. As she sat, she adjusted her light gray cotton dress adorned with colorful embroidered tulips. Wesley's grandmother's brooch sparkled in the bright Georgia sunlight. She was something to look at, all right!.

"Everyone, please settle down." She asked.

The adults sat on the benches that had been prepared for Molley's wedding, while the children gathered in front of them, sitting with their legs crossed on warm blankets. The rest of the adult children and soldiers stood behind the seated ones. The newlyweds were lying against an old live oak tree, cuddled in each other's arms, smiling and making goo-goo eyes.

"Well, obviously I've got some 'splainin' to do."

Many of the crowd giggled.

"I'm sure y'all have noticed that I've been spending a lot of my time with Lieutenant Jenkins, here." She looked at him with loving eyes. "And our time together has conceived a child that I'm carryin'."

Some cried out "Oh" or "Ah" in surprise and some merely shook their heads in discontent.

"I know, I know, this is scandalous indeed. And I…"

"I intend to make things right." Wesley interrupted her. "I'd like all of you to be my witness." He turned to Maggie Mae, got down on one knee, took her left hand and looked lovingly into her eyes. "Magnolia Mae Moon, will you do me the honor of becoming my wife?"

More oohs and ahhs were heard, and a few even cried out, "Oh, my!"

Maggie Mae was astonished by his move and the manner in which he proposed. She also looked at the group of people waiting for her answer—including her two children, who were smiling from ear to ear. This, of course, meant that they approved of his proposal. "Yes." She said quietly. Then louder: "Yes. I'll be your wife."

Everyone responded with applause, and the soldiers shouted their congratulations. Wesley quickly got up and kissed his bride-to-be. "You've made me the happiest man on earth. I love you so much! With all of me!"

"I love you with all of me—too!

Both Lizzie and Pauly ran up to their mother who was in Wesley's arms. "So, do we!"

Wesley kneeled again and said to Pauly: "You are the man of this house and I am making a promise to you that I will take care of your mother, no matter what, and I will give my life for her. Do you understand?"

"Yes, I do." He gave Wesley a warm hug.

"I'd also like to ask you to be my best man."

"You mean like you did with Molley's husband?"

"Yes, exactly."

"Then yes, I will be your best man." He shook Wesley's hand.

Wesley got up. "And as for you, young lady, what do you think of me as your stepfather?"

"I'd love that. I know Mama loves you, it's quite noticeable."

"Well, all right then…" he turned to Chesney, "…are you ready for another wedding?"

"I'm always ready fo' a weddin'!"

Everyone laughed loudly.

"So, when iz da baby due?" asked Molley.

Maggie Mae smiled. "Spring, I believe."

"Well, you know what they say?" Wesley asked.

"What?" Maggie Mae was puzzled.

"Good things always happen in springtime." Corporal Hughes exclaimed with a smile from ear to ear.

Everyone laughed boisterously.

"Everyone! Please quiet down. I've got a few more things to address." She sat back down and waited for the crowd to settle down. Wesley pulled up a chair and positioned himself next to her.

"Good. Well, I suppose I'm going to be wed." she smiled. "Rose, you already know that I'm gonna need you to create my gown for me."

"I cain't wait, Missy Maggie."

More happy sounds were heard from the crowd.

"All right, quiet down, please." She waited a few seconds. "As y'all may already imagine, this wedding is to be kept a secret."

Everyone became serious. They all were acutely aware of what would happen to all of them if this secret got out.

"Especially y'all young'ns, y'all gotta understand this weddin' is to be kept quiet. No talkin' with your friends from other plantations. Understand? This is very, very serious and very, very important. I am gonna give it to y'all straight, if any of them slaveowners find out about this, I will be lynched and y'all will be killed, in an instant. Are we clear?"

She felt she had gotten through to the younger children because their joy turned into fear. She saw that on their faces.

"Flora, I want you to start wearing larger clothes and as spring comes, I want you to wear a pillow."

"Why is dat, Missy Maggie?"

"Cause, you're gonna raise my child as your own."

The group gasped.

"Oh, I don't know if I can…"

"Yes, you can, and you will. I wouldn't trust anyone else with my child except my best friend in this whole world. That is you, Flora. You have been my friend ever since I can remember. Can I trust you with my child?"

"Yes'm, I'll take care of da boy or da girl. Whatever our Lord sends ya."

"Thank you, Flora. You are a dear friend." She got up and hugged her best friend. "Now, I've also thought about goin' into town."

"Dats gonna be a challenge."

"Yes, Charles, it will be, but I've got a plan. I'm gonna go into town until I can no longer go. I'm guessing 'bout January or February. I'm gonna buy double or triple the amount of staples that I usually buy and have the Potters deliver them here."

"What are ya gonna tell them folk? Dey is gonna git suspicious." Cato asked, concerned.

"I'll just say that I'm bedridden with a sickness and that I can't ride in a carriage."

"No, I don't like this plan. Sounds dangerous. What if they discover my men? Another battle will break out and I cannot have that. Not here, anyway."

Maggie Mae stayed silent. She knew her beloved was right, but she didn't have any other ideas.

"I know…what if we went to Atlanta instead of Valdosta?"

"Atlanta? Why dats gonna take a whole day's worth of travel and I don't tink das a gud idea since Missy Maggie is gonna be heavy by den."

"No, Charles, Willy has a good idea." She pointed to Fanny. "You'll come with us. Just in case somethin' happens, you will be there with me. You'll bring your things. It'll be risky but I do believe it can be done."

"Are you sure, Missy Maggie?" Fanny asked.

"Yes, Fanny, I'll be in your capable hands. I will be just fine."

Fanny nodded but she wasn't too sure about it.

"Good, now that's settled. Let's discuss the crops."

"What about them? We'll just have Mr. Banner buy them like he's done before."

"Yes, we can do that but…they haven't seen me in town much to sell my crop and if they continue to not see me, they're gonna start gossipin' about my plantation. Her crops must be goin' bad. She ain't growin' cotton no more. She ain't got no crop no more. Them negros got lazy and they ain't workin' no more." She paused. "I can just hear their venomous tongues now."

Many heads were nodding.

"Well, I'm not gonna let them gossip 'bout my plantation. When the flax is ready for market, I'm gonna sell it to the Valdosta market and take whatever they want to pay me for it."

"What if they ask about the cotton you sold to Mr. Banner?"

"Well, I'll tell them that my crop got some flea hoppers and they destroyed it. Simple. This way, they'll have pity on me and pay me more for the flax."

Wesley was impressed. She sure knew her stuff. He was beaming with pride for her.

"Is there anything I missed?"

"What 'bout deez 'ere Yanks? How you gonna explain dis if dey ax ya?"

"Good point, Ned." She rubbed her chin. "Any of ya got any ideas on Wesley's men?"

"Dysentery." Willy cried out.

"What about it?" asked Wesley.

"Well, ya cud say most of um caught it and passed on."

"Right. This way, if they come snooping around…"

"No, I will not let anyone come snooping around here. Look at what happened last time!"

"Right. Good point."

"I say, if anyone come 'round 'ere, we take care of dem jus' like last time."

"Yes, Charles, exactly my thought. Besides, they ain't comin' 'round anytime soon. I was very stern with the Sheriff. I warned him that if anyone came 'round again with those same intentions, I would not hesitate to protect my property again. I will **not** allow anyone to kill another member of my family."

"Yo' fierce, Missy Maggie." Cato commented.

Chapter Twenty-One

"What do you think about a Christmas wedding?"

"Oh, that would be lovely."

Wesley admired the brooch that Magnolia Mae was wearing. "It looks perfect on you, my love. My grandmother would have loved you." His finger slid up to her chin and he kissed her ever so lightly.

"She would?"

"Of course." He kissed her again, this time with a bit more feeling.

"Missy Maggie?" Rose approached. She had an idea.

"Yes, Rose, what is it?"

"I had an idea of da dress y'all be wearin' fo' yo' weddin'."

"Really?" she winked at Wesley and tilted her head.

"All right, well, I have things to do."

Wesley understood this cue for him to leave, and he quietly complied.

"All right then, he's gone. Do ya have an idea for my dress?"

"Yes'm." She took her mistress's hand and gently pulled her into the sewing room.

Maggie Mae didn't protest. Rather, she followed with delight as she knew well, from experience, that Rose would not disappoint.

"See, I took dis here gown from yo' mama's armoire." She gently lifted it from the hanger and lifted it with her other hand.

"Ah." Maggie Mae had always adored that gown. Her mother had worn it when she threw one of the most lavish Christmas parties Valdosta had ever seen. Most everyone was there, and most of the southern belles were extremely jealous of Rose's creation. Maggie Mae was twelve years old, but she was not too young to notice the envy and yearning in their eyes when they pretended to admire that dress. She recalled her mother in it, slowly descending the oak staircase, making absolutely sure that all her guests were present before making her entrance. Her figure was still quite slim, and her bosom was full and round. That day, Maggie Mae made a mental note that she was going to be just like her mother one day: vehement, brash, clamorous and proud. "I remember how mama looked in it. She was stunnin', wasn't she?"

"Yes'm, an' I tink it'll be perfect fa yo' weddin', 'specially since itz gonna be on Christmas day. Ya gon' need the warmth."

The outfit was made of heavy, scarlet, silk brocade with a white velvet ribbon adorning the waist, white velvet bows tying up each sleeve to the mid-arm, and a white velvet ribbon adorning the antebellum hemline. The jacket was a matching fabric, except that it was lined with pure white lapin. The same lapin adorned the neckline and ended with both sleeves festooned with the same white lapin. Rose had pierced several of her fingers sewing the lapin fur. Sewing the fur was a dreadful job, but in the end, it was all worth it. "Go on, Missy Maggie, try it on."

Magnolia Mae didn't have to be told twice. She dropped her grandmother's shawl on the floor and put on the jacket.

"Oh my! It'z perfect, yes'm!"

Maggie Mae viewed herself in the mirror that her father had bought her mother many years ago. "Yes, seems to fit perfectly, doesn't it?"

Rose pulled lightly on the back and brushed the collar. "Yes'm, it'z mighty fine, mighty fine. I don't need ta do nuttin to it." That was a big relief for her. She really did not want to touch it again.

"Yes, I agree. It doesn't need to be touched." She twirled in it a few times and then removed it. "Here. Now, let me try the dress."

"Here, lemme help ya." Rose began to unbutton the back of the forest green plaid wool dress Maggie was wearing and slipped it off. "Here." She picked up the red dress, which had already been prepared for the try-on, and slid it over her head. She shifted it into place and began buttoning it up. "Ah, I z tink it'z perfect. Dontcha?"

Maggie Mae couldn't believe what she saw. It was her mother's reflection in the mirror! Tears welled in her eyes. "Oh, Rose, dontcha see Mama?"

"Yes'm, I do. Why, I still remember dat day. She got fitted rat-chere in dis room…she was so pretty, she waz." She pulled out her handkerchief, dried her eyes, and sniffled. "What a pretty sight y'are Missy Maggie."

"Thank you Rose, and you know what…you don't have to fix anything on this gown and the jacket. They are perfect exactly as they are."

Rose was relieved. For once, she did not have to thread a needle. That outfit was perfect.

~~~~~~

"Are ya ready?" Charles was beaming with pride.

Maggie Mae took a deep breath. Her left arm hooked into Charles's and her right held a bouquet made up of small poinsettias that Harriet had grown on the side of the house. Every year George Terry would buy a large poinsettia for his beloved wife for Christmas and every year, Harriet would re-plant them on both sides of the house and every year they would bloom. This year, Harriet allowed Lizzie and Lana to pick all of them so to make up a bouquet for the bride and to adorn the same arch that they had used for Molley's wedding back in September. This time, they used garlands and ribbons from the Christmas decorations and decorated the chairs and benches that were once again set up in rows. The aisle was covered with red rose petals that Harriet and the younger girls had meticulously picked, dried, and stored solely for this wedding. The whole area looked like the parlor decorated for Christmas—except the white ceiling and crystal chandelier were replaced with a blue sky and a sparkling warm sun.

"Yes."

The music began and the march came shortly after. Magnolia Mae's joy was evident on her face. She smiled at each and every person standing and honoring her. "I so love these people, with all my heart," She quietly commented as she slowly marched by.

"And dey loves you, Missy Maggie. Oh, if only your parents were here."

"They are, Charles, they are."

"Yes'm." He smiled as they reached the altar. He grasped Wesley's hand and lightly kissed Maggie Mae on the cheek. Then he turned and took his seat next to his wife of almost fifty years.

"She's an angel." Harriet was genuinely happy for that sweet girl. "Her mama would be so proud."

"Yes, indeed."

This time the presider was Sergeant Blackwell. He was also the Chaplain for the Union brigade. "Very well. Let us begin. Dearly beloved, we are gathered together to unite this man and this woman in Holy Matrimony."

Sergeant Blackwell went on for several minutes, talking about Lieutenant Jenkins and Magnolia May Moon, and how they met. He detailed some of the obstacles they had to surmount, and how they were trendsetters. He explained how brave they were, given the Confederate mindset. Finally, he got to the magic words.

"Lieutenant Wesley Joshua Jenkins, do you take Magnolia Mae Terry Moon to be your lawfully wedded wife?"

"I do."

"And do you, Magnolia Mae Terry Moon, take Lieutenant Wesley Joshua Jenkins to be your lawfully wedded husband?"

"I do."

"Rings please."

Pauly pulled two wedding rings out of his small front vest pocket and handed them over to Sergeant Blackwell.

"Thank you, son." He gave the larger one to Maggie Mae and the smaller one to Wesley. She wanted to re-use Roland's wedding ring for Wesley, especially since she just could not go into town and buy new ones. Surely, she would get the third-degree from Mrs. Potters and the rest of the town gossipers.

"Lieutenant Jenkins, please place the ring on her finger and repeat after me. With this ring, I thee wed, to have and to hold until the end of time."

"With this ring, I thee wed, to have and to hold until the end of time." And he slid the ring on her finger.

"And now, your turn…"

Maggie Mae didn't need the words repeated, since she knew them very well. "With this ring, I thee wed, to have and to hold until the end of time." The ring was now Wesley's.

"And now, by the power vested in me, by the Union military and by the President of the United States, Abraham Lincoln, I declare you Man and Wife. You may kiss your bride."

They kissed intensely and lovingly—almost, but not quite, scandalously.

"Ladies and gentlemen, I am most proud to announce the newly married, Lieutenant and Mrs. Wesley Joshua Jenkins!"

The joy in the air could was palpable, just like the crisp, cool breeze wafting through the old Oak and Magnolia trees. Once again, festivities filled the brisk December air, warming it up with the blanket of love and family.

"Congratulations and Merry Christmas!" rang out, followed by loud, warm, applause.

~~~~~~

In early February, just as planned, Maggie Mae went into town to sell her flax crop, followed by Wesley, Charles and Sergeant Blackwell, perfectly disguised as slaves. Charles had schooled Blackwell to keep his head down and to never look any white person in the face. That was dangerous, and it surely would earn him a beating.

"Good mornin' gentlemen," she said as she walked by the usual iniquitous parties. She headed straight for Mr. Cooke, who stood up as soon as she approached.

"Mrs. Moon, you look as lovely as ever." He bowed, slightly, and doffed his hat.

"Well, bless yo' heart, Mr. Cooke. You always have such nice words to say." She extended her green gloved hand that matched her bonnet. Once again, Rose had been able to transform a dark and light green plaid dress with matching bolero to fit Maggie Mae's figure perfectly. She even left some wiggle room for the baby kicking inside her.

Mr. Cooke noticed something different about her, but he couldn't quite put his finger on it. Nonetheless, she was as magnificent and dignified as ever. *I'm going to give it another try.* He cleared his throat. "Mrs. Moon, I was wondering if you could do me the honor of having dinner with me," while not letting go of her hand.

Maggie Mae cringed, but she didn't move a muscle. Then she thought to play her cards to her advantage. "Well, Mr. Cooke, if we can strike a decent deal today, I might consider it."

Ah, good move, Wesley thought, while at the same time fuming with jealousy. *How dare that insipid human being make advances on my wife!* He clenched his fists.

Charles gently tugged on Wesley's jacket sleeve. He knew full well what was brewing inside, but that kind of insolence could get him killed, and he didn't want his Maggie Mae to become a widow again.

Mr. Cooke became aroused at the thought of entering the Valdosta Saloon with this gorgeous southern belle on his arm. "Well, all right then, let's take a look, shall we?" he motioned her to precede him.

"Here it is. What do y'all think?" she asked proudly.

Mr. Cooke took a good look around the wagon. "Oh, this is some mighty fine flax, yes indeed, mighty fine." He pulled his spectacles out of his front vest pocket and took a closer look at the crop in different spots. "Mighty fine, indeed." He was extraordinarily pleased with what he saw. "Let's go back inside, shall we, Mrs. Moon?"

"Of course." As she preceded him once again, she noticed her nemesis at the very back of the room, giving her the most snide and contemptuous of looks. She shuddered.

On the way home, Wesley and Maggie Mae sat together at the back of the wagon while Blackwell and Charles were sitting up in the driver's seat. Wesley was holding his wife in his arms as they kissed and laughed.

They were so busy paying attention to each other that they didn't notice the horse and buggy following them.

When they arrived at Magnolia Blossom, they headed for the barn where they stored the wagon until the next load of crop.

"Chesney, I hope you have dinner ready 'cause we iz famished."

"Yes'm, Missy Maggie, suppa iz reddi fo' y'all."

By the time they finished their supper, it was pitch dark outside, a bit chilly, with a moon shining brightly, like a diamond.

"Gentlemen, I'm goin' in. I'm gonna put this money away and then I'm headin' off to bed. I'm bushed."

"I'll be up in a few Darlin'. Just gonna finish this cigar."

"Take your time, Honey." She kissed her handsome husband on his forehead.

Magnolia Mae headed for the parlor, grabbed one of the pillows, pulled up the rug, knelt on the pillow, and opened the hatch to the hiding place. In her lapse, she failed to notice the shadowy figure lurking outside.

He watched as she lifted the cover of an opening in the floor. *Must be a hiding place,* he thought but kept perfectly still. She pulled out the dollars that Mr. Cooke had paid her earlier, counted them, and laid them by her side. He watched her pull some sort of metal box from a hiding place, remove a small key from her bosom, and open the box. His eyes widened. *Look at all that cash! So, that's where that dirty negro-lover kept his money!* He attentively watched as she counted several hundred dollars. Then she placed the money she had earned earlier and added it to the pile in the box. She marked something on a piece of paper, closed the box, locked it, and placed it back inside the hiding place.

"There," she said as she got up. As she was about to cover the hiding place with the rug, a hard pounding came from the front door—so hard, it could be heard throughout the entire house. "Well now, who could that be?" she opened the door and found herself looking at the barrel of Mr. Hart's pistol.

"You connivin', lyin', killin', negro lovin' bitch!" Benjamin yelled as he stepped inside. "Now, ya gon' pay fo' killin' my only son!"

"I will not let you hurt my wife, Hart!"

"Yo' wife?" Hart was incredulous. He couldn't believe his eyes or ears. "Wife? You is a negro! You cain't marry no white woman!" he lifted his pistol and aimed right between Wesley's eyes. "Well, I'm gonna fix dis 'ere situation right now." He moved closer to Maggie Mae.

"First, I'm gonna kill y'all, den I'm gonna take dis here plantation and make it mine!" he got close enough that the end of the pistol was only a foot away from Maggie Mae's head. "I'm gonna start with you and end with the youngest negro on dis here plantation."

"You leave her be! She didn't kill your son, I did!" Wesley rushed to stand in front of his wife putting his face right in front of the end of Hart's pistol.

"I knew it! Yo' ain't a southern negro, yo' is a Yankee negro…well…well…well…you an' your wife here are gonna die tagedda tonight." He cocked the hammer.

Suddenly, a shot rang out, and Hart's forehead had a hole that started bleeding as he collapsed to the floor. Both Wesley and Maggie Mae turned to see Sergeant Blackwell pointing her favorite pistol in Hart's direction.

"Oh, my Lord, thank you Sergeant!" she cried out as she let Wesley cuddle her in his arms.

"He must have been following us."

"And we didn't notice." Wesley looked at the dead body. "How did we miss that? He could have killed any one of us!"

"Well, he didn't"

The entire family huddled together in the hallway next to the kitchen, shaking at the sight of the dead, southern white man.

"Is everyone all right?"

"Yes, tank da Lord!" Harriet cried out.

"We need to get this vermin body out of our house, now!" came the instruction from Wesley. So, he and Sergeant Blackwell wrapped Hart's body in a white sheet and dragged it outside.

No one slept well that night. The next morning, Wesley and Sergeant Blackwell, placed Hart's body into his buggy. They hitched his horse to the back of the Terrys' coach. Maggie Mae was wearing a heavy wool overcoat on top of her burgundy dress. Her hat, gloves and shoes were all black, in honor of the deceased body that was riding behind her. They headed into town and stopped right in front of Sherriff Coulter's office.

As the sheriff strode out of the office, He frowned as he announced to no one in particular, "Well, well, well. What do we have here?" He could well imagine what had happened.

"Sheriff."

"Good mornin', Mrs. Moon." He tipped his hat.

"Mr. Benjamin Hart followed me home last evenin' and was peekin' through my window while I was storin' my crop earnins. He forced himself into my home and he threatened me and…" she cried on his chest as he held her tight. "Why couldn't he just leave me be? Why? I neva did nothin' to him. He accused me of killin' James, but I did not…" she wailed. "It was Melton, he shot him just before he got shot and died!" then she sniffled, dried her eyes, and turned very serious. "I warned him, I warned everyone that if anyone dared to attack me again, I would defend myself. I told y'all."

"Well, all right now. Come inside, all of ya."

They all followed the sheriff into his small office. There were only a couple of chairs, an old wood bench against the wall, and a small jail cell. He sat in his chair and removed his hat. "Now, I'm gonna start with you Charles. Tell me exactly what happened." He plunged his pen into the ink bottle and prepared to write Charles's account on paper.

"Well, Sheriff, itz egzaclee as Missy Maggie said, he dun come in demandin' her money and she gotz her daddy's pistol and shot him, she did."

"Where's the pistol?"

"Ratch 'ere." Wesley handed it to the Sheriff, who sniffed the end of the barrel.

"Yep, bin shot." He looked at Wesley and Blackwell. "Is she tellin' the truth boys?"

They both nodded without saying a word.

The Sheriff took a deep breath and sighed. "Oh well, sign here, then, all of ya, and then y'all can leave."

Maggie Mae signed her name properly and the rest of the men, signed with a cross. They all left silently, mounted the coach, and took off back toward Magnolia Blossom.

The Sheriff put his hat on and headed for the undertaker, shaking his head in near disbelief. "Dang woman!"

~~~~~~

"Lieutenant! Lieutenant! I have a telegram for you!"

"Not right now, soldier! Can't you see I'm busy?" Wesley barked at the young soldier. He had been pacing up and down the corridor for what seemed like hours.

"Please, Lieutenant! you must read this telegram!" he pushed the piece of paper closer to Wesley.

"Fine!" he snatched it, unfolded it, and read it. His eyes were wide with amazement.

The cry of a newborn pierced the silence. Both men turned their heads toward Maggie Mae's bedroom. Charles rushed up the stairs as soon as he heard the cry. Only ten minutes had passed, but to Wesley, it seemed like an eternity. The door finally opened, and Fanny came out cleaning her hands on her apron.

"It'z a boy! A beautiful baby boy! And he's screamin' good an' healthy!"

Wesley let out a sigh of relief.

"Congratulations, Lieutenant!" Charles shook his hand.

"Yo' iz a father now. Yo' iz a man now. Yo' ain't no boy no mo.'"

"Thank you, Charles." He gave him a very tight, bear hug.

"Now, go on in. Yo'son is awaitin'." Fanny commanded.

Wesley slowly opened the door and walked in. In bed was a mother sweating, with soaking wet curls, but a bright smile on her face holding a light, mocha-shaded newborn. Harriet went toward the door and stopped in front of Wesley.

"He so beautiful! Looks jus' like ya!" she hugged the young father and left the room.

"Well, don't just stand there. Come and meet your son." Maggie Mae smiled warmly at her anxious husband. "Don't be afraid. He won't bite. He ain't got no teeth yet."

For a moment, Wesley's legs would not move. But when his wife extended her hand towards him, his body nearly floated in her direction. He got down on one knee so he could see his son in a better light. "He's…he's…"

"Yours…ours…isn't he beautiful?"

Wesley was so choked up he could only nod.

"Would you like to hold him?"

"Yes," he said faintly. He took the bundle in his arms and sat on the bed, gazing at his son who yawned while making a funny face. Wesley was in awe.

"So, what are we naming him?"

Wesley thought of the news he just heard. "Liber." He paused. "Liber Abe Jenkins."

"Liber?"

"It means free in Latin."

"Free? Why would you want to call him free?"

"Because he's free. The war is over. The North won. All black people are free now."

"Oh, my goodness!" she started to cry. "April 9, 1865 will be a day that we will never forget." She kissed her son's head.

"No, we won't."

As an indie... (independent) author...

I rely on reviews. In fact, those gold stars are indie authors' lifelines. If you truly care about your favorite indie author, please leave a review on at least one of the following websites:

Amazon - www.Amazon.com

Barnes & Noble - www.barnesandNoble.com

BookBub - www.Bookbub.com

Goodreads - www.Goodreads.com

Google Books - https://play.google.com

iBooks App - https://iBooks.com

Thank you so much for your support. Please, don't forget—I write for you!

Your favorite author,

Joanne Fisher

Joanne's Next Book— Christmas in Florence

And now please enjoy a preview from Joanne's next Christmas novella, titled *"Christmas in Florence"*

~~~~~

"Hey, ma, guess what? I found a job!"

"Oh, Dante, that's wonderful! I'm so happy for you." Sofia hugged her son. "Now, sit and tell me all about it while I make some espresso."

Dante sat down and noticed a batch of biscotti that his mom just pulled out of the oven. "Mmmm…hey ma, can I have one?"

"Of course, Dante, go for it." She set up the espresso pot, turned on the heat and went to sit next to her son. "Now, tell me all about it." Her smile extended from ear to ear.

Dante had graduated from Humber College in fall of 2019 and had been searching for his career position ever since. He had many offers, but he wanted to find a position where he could travel to Italy. He was interested in perfecting his Italian. Even if he grew up in Woodbridge, he still spoke very little Italian. The only Italian he spoke was Calabrese dialect when he talked to his grandmother. Since his Nonna Teresa passed in 2018, his opportunities to speak Italian diminished drastically.

Sofia was so proud of her Dante. He was the oldest and most responsible and dependable of all her children. She really wanted him to be happy, but she would have settled for him to have a job that kept him closer to her, but he didn't want that. Ever since he was in middle school, he desired to fly the coop.

"All right, well this company is called LCD which means Leather Commerce Distributor and they are located in Calgary."

"Calgary? That's so far away, Dante." Horrified, she slapped her own face with her right hand.

"Ma, I'm not going to Calgary, it's just their headquarters. They have offices all over Canada, all right?"

Sofia nodded and kept quiet.

"They basically sell leather hides to countries that produce leather goods like jackets, handbags, shoes and so on."

"Shoes? You've piqued my interest."

Dante rolled his eyes. What was it with women and shoes? "Anyway, they were looking for a point of contact to travel to Italy and since I'm Italian, they hired me."

Sofia didn't know whether to laugh or cry. She frowned instead. "Italy huh?"

"Ma, come on, you knew I was looking for something like this. I want to travel, and I want to become fluent in Italian. This is exactly what I've been looking for. I've told you this over and over." He was losing his temper. His mother was way overprotective.

"I know, Dante, I know but you know how it is? We're Italian and we don't like our kids leaving home, not now, not ever." She sipped her espresso. "But I understand that you've always wanted to leave, so now's your chance. Bravo." She sounded very annoyed.

"Ma, come on, I'm gonna be thirty this year!"

"Yeah, yeah, thirty…So, when are you leaving?"

"End of this month."

"So soon?"

"Yeah." He cracked a smile. The excitement made his eyes light up. "I got a feeling that 2020 is gonna be a hell of a year."

Made in the USA
Columbia, SC
27 June 2024